THE SECRET COURIER

PART I

An Untold Gripping WW2 Historical Fiction of the Heroic British Spy Who Helped Win World War II

(Based on a True Story)

CURT O'RILEY

Copyright © 2024 Curt O'Riley.

All rights reserved. No part of this book may be used or reproduced in any form whatsoever without written permission except in the case of brief quotations in critical articles or reviews.

This book is a work of fiction. Names, characters, businesses, organizations, places, events and incidents either are the product of the author's imagination or are used fictitiously. Any resemblance to actual persons, living or dead, events, or locales is entirely coincidental.

ALSO BY THE AUTHOR

WORLD WAR II HOLOCAUST FICTION SERIES

WORLD WAR II HOLOCAUST FICTION SERIES

CONTENTS

CHAPTER ONE 7

CHAPTER TWO 16

CHAPTER THREE 24

CHAPTER FOUR 30

CHAPTER FIVE 36

CHAPTER SIX 42

CHAPTER SEVEN 45

CHAPTER EIGHT 52

CHAPTER NINE 63

CHAPTER TEN 71

CHAPTER ELEVEN 82

CHAPTER TWELVEE 87

CHAPTER THIRTEEN 96

CHAPTER FOURTEEN 101

CHAPTER FIFTEEN 107

THE SECRET COURIER

CHAPTER SIXTEEN 117

CHAPTER SEVENTEEN 125

CHAPTER EIGHTEEN 129

CHAPTER NINETEEN 138

CHAPTERTWENTY 146

CHAPTER TWENTY-ONE 156

CHAPTER TWENTY-TWO 164

CHAPTER TWENTY-THREE 168

CHAPTER TWENTY-FOUR 174

CHAPTER TWENTY-FIVE 182

CHAPTER TWENTY-SIX 189

CHAPTER TWENTY-SEVEN 194

AUTHOR NOTE 201

RECOMMENDED READS 202

ABOUT THE AUTHOR 203

THE SECRET COURIER

" *Bound by duty to secrets keep,*

Yet fate, in irony, does steep."

1

CHAPTER ONE

Olivia awakened abruptly, sitting straight up in bed. She wiped the beads of perspiration from her forehead and looked at the clock on the wall... 12 a.m. As she got up, the blankets that had encircled her minutes before tumbled to the floor in a moist, sweaty mess. She walked to the bathroom, turned on the light, and examined herself in the mirror for a bit. Dark circles lingered under her bloodshot eyes, and her face was pallid from fatigue. She turned on the faucet and sprayed cold water on her face. She wiped her face with the sleeve of her nightgown and checked her look once again. She sighed and turned off the light before stepping back into the bedroom. Picking up the sheets from the floor, she lay down again.

THE SECRET COURIER

Olivia had been awakened by the same dream numerous times before, and it had returned tonight. It was the same summer day, with the same warm July breeze that had touched her face four months before... She had watched, motionless, as her father and brother were carried from their house. And had awakened to the sound of gunfire, like she had always done.

She'd never forget that day. The day her father and brother were killed by the Gestapo. She and her sister had seen their father, Maxwell, and brother, Harrison, hauled into the street and shot. Olivia had awakened almost every night since that day to the sound of the same gunshot, and the nightmares had only worsened since her sister had gone.

It had been over a month since Grace went for England. And, although her leaving was Olivia's choice, not Grace's, she grieved for the companionship she had lost the instant her sister boarded the train. Especially evenings like this one, when she was left alone with the same thoughts and memories that tortured her.

Olivia turned over in bed, her gaze fixed on the softly lit starry night sky outside the window. It had been 4 months. The green leaves that had decorated the trees four months before had become vivid yellows and oranges and fallen to the ground, leaving barren limbs in their place.

The pleasant air that enveloped her that July night has been replaced by the harsh cold of November. Time had flown by so quickly. It had continued as if her world had not been wrecked. As if she hadn't lost almost everything she loved.

She knew something like this might happen. They all did. Almost two years ago, her father volunteered his services to the British Secret Intelligence Service. When he did, he accepted the associated risk.

Olivia was just 19 years old when they learned about Germany's invasion of Poland. Her father had foreseen that Holland would soon be conquered as well. He'd made a deal with the British SIS. In exchange for his spying, Olivia and Grace would get new identities and safe passage to London. She and her sister had assumed their mother's maiden name, Carter... Their father and brother had not been as fortunate. When the Dutch were obliged to register under the new German authority, her father and brother registered as Kensington, earning them the yellow star that all Jewish men, women, and children would soon be required to wear.

Olivia reflected about that day.

THE SECRET COURIER

"Grace... Grace! We need to relocate. W-We need to go!" She grabbed her sister and yanked her away from the window where they had been watching the events unfold.

Grace was locked in place, the effects of shock overwhelming her body. Olivia dragged her sister down the stairs, attempting to maintain her calm. She couldn't break down. Not until she was sure her sister was secure. Only then would she allow herself to fall beneath the weight of what had occurred.

"Grace, Grace!" Listen to me." She grasped her sister's shoulders tightly. "We need to go! We cannot remain here. Do you hear me? We need to go to the safehouse!"

Olivia shoved the memories aside. If something happened to their father, they were told to travel to a safe place and wait for his extraction. They had followed his instructions and had been apprehended by SIS operatives only hours later. They were transferred to the adjacent city of Leiden, where they languished for over three months before receiving what was promised: two tickets aboard a steamship bound for London. However, she had been unable to escape. She couldn't allow her father's and brother's efforts, as well as their deaths, go in vain. So, she decided to remain behind and act as a spy herself. They looked at her like she was insane when she made the offer, but they

THE SECRET COURIER

agreed nevertheless.

She had stayed in Leiden till the day her sister left. After she and Grace said their goodbyes, Harold and Cecilia Winslow, the SIS agents she would be working with, took her back to Den Haag. They'd transferred her to a modest cottage on the outskirts of town.

She was pleased she didn't have to return home. The notion of witnessing the location where her father and brother were killed made her sick to her stomach. Once settled there, the Winslows started about getting her a job. Her appointment had just arrived three days before; she would be working as a secretary for General Gunther Sinclair, the leader of the German War Office in Holland. She was set to start in a week.

Olivia sat upright in bed. It seems that she wouldn't be sleeping tonight. She rose and walked to the door of her bedroom. She opened it and proceeded down the hallway to the living room, which shared space with the kitchen and dining area. She couldn't recall the last time she had slept all night. Honestly, that had probably happened before the conflict.

She went to the sink, took a glass from the cabinet above, and filled it. She turned, leaning against the counter, and gulped a few gulps of water. She reflected about her youth... the cottage she currently resided in reminded her of the house she and her family had shared when Olivia was a youngster. Every night, her mother would carry Olivia and her sister to their room. Every night, she would bring them cups of warm milk and tell them a bedtime tale. Every night, until Olivia was twelve.

She could still remember the brilliant red rash that had covered her mother's weak body after typhoid illness had killed her. Her father soon relocated Olivia and her siblings to the city. Olivia set her cup down on the table and grabbed the tea kettle from the stove top. If there was one thing she had learnt in the last several years, it was that a strong cup of tea could solve everything. She filled the kettle by turning on the tap again.

A loud bang at the door caused Olivia to drop the kettle onto the burner. She turned, her gaze fixed on the front door. Who may be knocking on her door at this hour? More importantly, what did they want? A big boom echoed again. Whoever it was, they wanted in. She quickly grabbed her purse from the dining room table and drew out the hidden handgun. She moved slowly towards the door. She reached out and carefully twisted the knob, the door groaning as it opened. She looked around, her weapon aimed squarely in front of her. There was no one present.

"Hello?" She shouted out into the darkness.

"P-please, he-help me," A voice called back. She glanced down and gasped. A guy lay at her feet. He was German. The appearance of his clothing suggests that he is a captain. Olivia positioned her revolver in the direction of the stranger, her finger on the trigger.

The guy had been injured, and his green suit was saturated with his own blood. She searched the darkness for anybody else. They were alone. She stepped back. He was a German soldier. She leveled her rifle at the guy once again. She could and should murder him. The Germans would blame it on the Dutch resistance. They were presumably the ones that shot him initially. Nobody would ever know the difference.

She put her finger on the trigger. After a lengthy time, she dropped her weapon and stepped back, running a hand over her hair.

"God, please do it... What is wrong with you?" she thought as she looked back at the guy, whose breathing had become labored. She sighed in frustration and returned her rifle on the table before kneeling next to the soldier. He was still alive, very barely. She linked her arms under his, causing faint gasps from the guy as she attempted to draw him within.

Olivia turned him over. "Oh God..." she muttered, taking in his

THE SECRET COURIER

state. He'd been shot in the abdomen. She rushed to the medicine cabinet. No antiseptic. Damn. She turned, opened the next cupboard, and grabbed a half-empty bottle of Gin. She placed the bottle down on the table and hurried to the end table next to the couch, where she took out a sewing kit from the drawer. She took the Gin off the table and knelt next the guy. She set to work unbuttoning his coat and then his shirt.

She removed the bloodied clothing and checked the wound. Blood was still streaming from it. If it wasn't closed, he would bleed out. She grabbed the bottle of Gin and unscrewed the top with her teeth while holding it under pressure with a towel.

"This is going to sting." She lifted the cloth from the incision and poured the contents of the bottle over it. The guy moaned in anguish but did not move. Olivia took a needle and thread from the sewing kit that lay beside her. She took a big breath. She stitched the wound edges together with a trembling hand. After a few minutes of labor, she stepped back to examine her work. She lacked a surgeon's competence, yet her suturing was effective. Most of the bleeding had ceased. She took in a long breath and let it out with a sigh. The guy was unconscious but alive.

She rose up and walked to the medical cabinet, returning with a handful of gauze, some tape, and a bottle of Morphine. She began dressing the newly sutured incision, covering it with many layers of gauze before fastening it with tape. She raised the man's head and placed the bottle of Morphine to his lips.

"It's not much, but it'll help," she murmured, not knowing why she was speaking to an unconscious person, and poured some morphine into the man's mouth. She rocked back, sitting on her bottom and leaning on the leg of the kitchen table.

She let out an annoyed groan and ran her hands through her hair, watching the man's chest rise and fall with each feeble breath. Had she just made a major error?

THE SECRET COURIER

2

CHAPTER TWO

"You're awake."

Olivia entered into her house's spare bedroom to discover the German soldier she had been caring for straining to sit up, eyes heavy with tiredness, forehead beaded with new drops of perspiration from the energy his attempts to rise from the bed he was in had required.

"Don't try to get up," Olivia urged, sitting down with the tray she had been holding on the bedside table.

"You'll bust your stitches," she said, crouching alongside him and gently lowering him back onto his back.

"Wh-what happened?" The guy said in a throaty whisper, his eyes fixed on Olivia.

"You were shot..." Olivia remarked warily, looking at the guy.

"Am I in an h-hospital?"

"No," Olivia said, shaking her head.

"I discovered you at my doorstep. I have been taking care of you here." She collected the tray she had been carrying when she stepped in and placed it at the foot of the bed before sitting on the bedside stool.

"Are you a nurse?" The soldier inquired, studying her more attentively as she went about opening and prepping the different things that littered the tray.

"No," Olivia said, opening the bottle of Morphine and putting a little quantity into a measuring cup.

"Drink this. "It will relieve the pain," she remarked, handing out the cup.

"I'm fine," the guy said, looking at the dark, viscous liquid with caution.

"It wasn't a suggestion," she emphasized, placing the cup right in front of his face.

"Besides, you'll wish you had it once I'm done cleaning your wound." The man's gaze shifted from the cup to Olivia, then back to the cup. He reached out gingerly and grabbed it, putting

THE SECRET COURIER

the contents into his lips and swallowed with a grimace.

"Good." She grabbed the cup from him and put it back on the tray.

"Now," Olivia said, reaching for the buttons on the man's shirt, "I'll need to redress your wound." The guy nodded, wincing as he lay back on the mattress.

Olivia peeled up the white button-down she had clothed the soldier in after removing his bloodied uniform. The shirt had belonged to her brother and suited the guy well, but the length was a little short on his body due to his height being a few inches higher than Harrison's. Olivia studied the bandage she had applied to the man's abdomen, gently peeling aside the medical tape she had used to fasten it. She slowly peeled aside the gauze. The incision seemed clean; with the improvised sutures she had sewed in place firmly keeping the wound's borders together.

The gunshot wound was bigger than she had anticipated the night she discovered him. The culprit most likely used a shotgun of some type, maybe a rifle. A firearm could not have done as much harm to this guy. She gently stroked her finger across the sutures. He required almost ten to fill up the full hole caused by

18

THE SECRET COURIER

the bullet. Olivia looked up at the soldier's face. He was observing her with fascination. She quickly drew her hand away, a hot flush rising across her cheeks.

She took a bottle of Gin off the tray. The guy wrinkled his brow, a confused expression on his face.

"No rubbing alcohol on hand I'm afraid." Olivia shrugged.

"I've been using this to clean your wound." Twisting off the cap, she carefully tilted the bottle over, taking care to just pour a tiny quantity over the wound. The man's face wrinkled up in anguish, and his abdominal muscles contracted.

"Sorry," Olivia murmured, smiling regretful as she recapped the bottle and returned it on the tray. She took a gauze and patted the wound dry.

"So," the guy said, gritting his teeth as Olivia wiped at the painful area. "If you aren't a nurse, how do you know how to suture?" he moaned in misery.

"My father was a doctor," Olivia said absentmindedly, taking a dry gauze and laying it over the spot before taping it. "I helped in his clinic when I was younger."

"Where is he now?" The guy inquired, his muscles loosening now that she had done her task.

"Was he enlisted as an army medic?"

"No..." Olivia answered, her face tinged with grief as the memories of her father's death came flooding back. She gulped and pushed the thoughts aside.

"He died. Died in a car accident with my brother," she claimed. She met the soldier's gaze.

He looked at her, his face wrinkled with astonishment and anxiety.

"I ..." He continued, but then trailed off, "I'm sorry." Olivia offered him a sorrowful grin.

"It's okay," she responded with a dismissive wave of her head. "It was a long time ago." She averted her eyes, feeling uneasy in the man's presence.

"Do you feel like eating? She inquired, shifting the topic.

"I'm starving," the guy said with a nod of his head. She nodded back.

"I'll bring you some broth." Olivia stood and picked up the tray before exiting the room. She reappeared a minute later, tray in hand, with a little dish of hot liquid on top. She set it on the man's lap and helped move him into a sitting posture, supporting him with cushions before returning to her seat.

"That's not much. Just some bone broth. I don't want to put your stomach to the test just yet, especially since you've been sleeping for three days." The guy stared at her with a bewildered expression.

"Three days?" The guy inquired; his face furrowed. Olivia nodded.

"You came down with a fever the morning after I found you ... nearly 103," she went on to say.

"I have lots of morphine, but no antibiotics. So, all I could do was keep your wound clean and hope the fever subsided on its own. However, that did not happen until this morning." She added. He nodded, but his brow remained furrowed.

"Well..." she started, rising to her feet again. "I'll leave you to your meal." When the guy spoke, she turned to face the door and stopped in its frame.

"I don't believe I caught your name." Olivia turned to face him, laying her hand on the doorframe. Should she lie? Tell him the truth, or at least her twisted interpretation of the truth. She couldn't give him her true name, of course.

"Olivia," she said, deciding that the truth, no matter how bent, was her best choice. "Olivia Carter." The guy nodded, and for the first time a faint grin appeared on his lips. "I don't believe I caught yours either," she said, matching his grin.

"Hans Friedrich," the guy answered.

"Well," Olivia replied, her grin expanding. "It's nice to meet you,

Mr. Friedrich."

"Likewise ... Ms. Carter."

***

Olivia turned the doorknob to the guest bedroom. She cracked it open and glanced inside. The soldier had fallen asleep with the tray still on his lap.

She went inside after fully opening the door. She scooped up the tray from his lap and placed it on the bureau. As she turned towards the entrance, something grabbed her attention. She returned her gaze to the desk, focusing on the man's uniform jacket. Something was glinting in the afternoon sunshine streaming through the window. She unfurled the jacket, checking over her shoulder to ensure he was still sleeping, and saw a sparkling medal attached to the front pocket.

A Knight's Cross! Olivia unpinned the medal and lifted it up to inspect. The front shield was bloodstained, as was most of his other clothes. She licked her thumb and rubbed it over the medal, smearing the dried blood and restoring its shininess. Though she understood nothing about German military medals, she did know that a Knight's Cross was not bestowed to just anybody.

She returned her attention to the soldier laying in bed,

clutching his medal tenderly in her hands. Hans. He had said that his name was Hans. He seemed nice... what did such a purportedly decent guy accomplish to get a medal from the German Reich? What had he done that the Nazi government considered 'honorable'? Olivia shoved the thoughts aside. Of course, he was nice to her; she had saved his life. But what if he knew the truth? Would he be as sympathetic to her?

What if he knew she was everything the Nazis despised the most? Olivia turned and placed the medal on the bureau. She had forgotten herself before. She forgot who she was dealing with. Hans could show her all the tenderness in the world, but it wouldn't erase who he was... or the danger he represented.

3

CHAPTER THREE

"Scheisse," Hans muttered in German, as Olivia poured the remaining gin bottle contents over his wound.

"Sorry," Olivia said, rubbing the wound dry with gauze. It had mended wonderfully throughout Hans's ten-day stay in her care. The bright red, inflammatory tissue had began to become pink, and he had not had any more fevers.

Olivia's discovery of the Knight's Cross served as a wake-up call, and she determined to maintain her distance from the soldier ever since, only entering his chamber to bring him food and drink or heal his wound.

Sure, she hadn't let him die after discovering him on her doorstep, but something told Olivia that if her secret was found, it would be of little consequence to the German Reich... or Hans for that matter.

"It's hard to believe you're not a nurse," Hans murmured, observing her as she loaded all of her equipment onto a tray. "You've never thought about becoming one?"

"Actually, I have," Olivia said, a faint grin spreading over her lips at the thought. "I had plans to go to London and study at the Nightingale School of Nursing there," she said, her grin dimming. "That was before the war of course."

"War changes everything," Hans said absently.

After a lengthy, uncomfortable pause, Olivia cleared her throat: "What about you? What were you doing before the war? Or were you always a military man?"

Hans laughed. "I don't think you'd believe me if I told you."

Olivia grinned. "Try me."

"I... was studying to become... an accountant," Hans said, waiting for her reply. Olivia pursed her lips, unable to contain the giggle that threatened to escape her.

"An accountant ... that's ..." She started, but he stopped her off.

"Dull?" He grinned at her.

"Well, I wasn't going to put it so plainly," she said, giggling.

THE SECRET COURIER

"My father's been an accountant for nearly forty years so it just made sense to follow in the family business..." Hans started, then trailed off.

"I suppose war does change everything," Olivia remarked.

"I suppose it does," Hans said.

Olivia began collecting the remainder of her materials, hoping to fill the hole of uncomfortable stillness that had returned to the room.

"I'll bring you some dinner," she said, putting the top back on the empty gin bottle and setting it on the tray she was carrying. Hans did not speak again until she had risen up and turned to face the door.

"I really wish you'd stay this time."

Olivia paused in her position, unsure what to do next.

"I've been here for ten days and I've only seen you for a handful of minutes," he said. He was observing her. She could feel his gaze digging into her back. She gulped and turned on her heels to face him.

"I thought you could use the extra rest," she said in jest. Her rationale for spending so little time in his room had nothing to do with getting enough rest. She, of course, had purposefully kept her distance from him.

26

THE SECRET COURIER

"Well," Hans continued, sitting up in bed, "I feel a lot more rested. And I'd want some company for supper."

Olivia hesitated. She had spent barely a few minutes with him since he awoke a week earlier.

Would a single dinner together really damage anything?

"Well," Olivia eventually said, "You seem to be feeling better. I guess we could eat in the kitchen... if you feel like it."

"I would like that," Hans said, throwing the covers back and struggling to get up.

"Oh, here, let me help you," Olivia set the dish down and helped Hans rise up by wrapping an arm around him and placing a hand under his arm.

"Take it nice and slow," she said, going a few feet behind him till he sat at the kitchen table.

"Thank you," Hans said as Olivia placed a plate of food in front of him.

"You're welcome," she said, taking a seat with her plate. It wasn't much, simply porridge and bread, but Hans looked satisfied with it. In fact, he looked relieved to get out of the chamber where he had been imprisoned for over two weeks.

"So do you have any brothers and sisters?" She inquired, choosing to initiate conversation.

Hans smiled and nodded: "A younger brother and sister."

THE SECRET COURIER

"Do they live at home with your parents?"

He shook his head. "My sister does. My brother was called up at the same time as I was." He stopped, his grin dimming. "He died in France ... nearly two years ago now."

"Oh..." Olivia blinked and looked away. "I'm sorry."

"He died an honorable death," Hans said calmly, as if he had practiced the statement a hundred times. Olivia nodded and prodded at the food on her plate.

"He would've been about your age," Hans said, glancing up at her. "You are what? twenty-two, twenty-three?"

"Twenty-two," Olivia said. Hans nodded absently.

"My brother ... he would've been about your age now."

Hans riveted his gaze on her, as if he had seen her for the first time since their talk began.

"And my sister," Olivia said, holding the gold locket around her neck. She unclasped it and held it out to Hans, revealing a fading black and white portrait of her sister enclosed inside the oval case. "Grace ... She's seventeen."

"Where is your sister now?" He inquired, taking the locket in his fingers and quickly examining it before giving it to her.

"England," Olivia said, closing the clasp and placing the chilly metal to her breast.

THE SECRET COURIER

"My father thought fourteen was too young for the horrors of war, so he sent her away to live with relatives back in '39," she said. After all, she couldn't risk saying too much. Especially knowledge that may put her sole remaining family at jeopardy.

"Your father was right," Hans said, forcing Olivia to glance up from her meal. "I said the same thing about my brother when he decided to enlist ... and he was twenty." He remembered the incident with a sour grin on his face.

"I suppose it doesn't matter how old they are, when it comes to someone you care about," Olivia answered, mirroring his sour grin. If she had gotten her way, her sister would have been transported to England at the start of the war. Despite Olivia's efforts to hide her from it all, Grace had seen so much. Much more than a 17-year-old should.

Hans gave a slight grin, "I suppose not."

THE SECRET COURIER

4

CHAPTER FOUR

"You what?!" Olivia was sitting in the living room when a voice roared out. She had gone home at nightfall to meet with Harold and Cecilia Winslow, the SIS agents she was supposed to report to. Olivia had housed a German army commander for over two weeks and decided it was time to be straight with the couple, a move she now regretted.

"What was I supposed to do? Let him bleed to death in front of my door?" Olivia fired back, defensively, at Harold's accusing tone.

"It would've bloody beat nursing him back to health like a sick

THE SECRET COURIER

puppy," Harold said as he paced around the room. Olivia gave a frustrated sigh.

"I would appreciate it if you stopped treating me like some disillusioned child."

"Then stop acting like one!" He bit back. "What? Do you believe he would have done the same for you? You don't suppose if he knew who you were, he would have given you into the wicked Gestapo or shot you himself?"

Of course, I don't! But he doesn't know who I am, right?

Harold huffed and turned away from her to resume pacing.

"Harv, maybe she has a point," Cecilia spoke for the first time since Olivia had revealed the news. She continued despite Harold's confused and annoyed expression. "Think about it. A German officer is found dead on the doorstep of a girl who is just two weeks away from starting a career at the War Office. Don't you believe that would create more questions than the current situation?"

Harold's brow wrinkled as he considered Cecilia's statements.

"Also, the route he was on is extensively used by soldiers heading north. I'm sure he'll be on his way someplace far away in a few days, and we'll be able to forget about the entire thing," Cecilia said, turning to Olivia.

31

THE SECRET COURIER

"Has he said where exactly he was heading?"

Olivia shakes her head. "I didn't ask."

Cecilia nodded. "Well if he's a captain like you say, I'm sure he's headed somewhere much more important than Den Haag."

"In the meantime, I want you keeping your distance from him, do you understand?" Harold cut in.

"I have been," Olivia said sadly.

"Well," Harold focused his gaze on Olivia. "At least you've been doing something right."

***

Olivia pulled her cloak tightly about her, her dark auburn locks blowing in the biting, winter wind. She hadn't expected her meeting with the Winslows to go any better than it did, but Harold treating her as if she were a dumb kid still irritated her.

Walking up the stairs to her home, she struggled with the key in her gloved hand before pushing it into the door. She snapped it open, enjoying the warmth that rushed her face as she walked inside. Olivia jumped as she heard a chair scraping on the hardwood floor. Hans, who had been seated at the kitchen table, was now standing in front of her.

"Oh, I didn't realize you were up," she responded hurriedly.

THE SECRET COURIER

"Sorry, I didn't mean to scare you," he said, taking a step forward. "I just couldn't take another second alone in that room," he said, indicating down the hall towards the spare bedroom.

"I'm sorry," she said, placing her gloves into the pockets of her coat before pulling it off. "I popped out to go to the grocery store," she said, putting her coat on a rack near the entrance.

"Do you need help?" Hans asked.

"Help with what?"

"... Bringing the ... groceries in?" Hans answered, his face furrowed in perplexity.

"Oh," Olivia muttered, looking around. "Turns out," she said, grabbing for the tiny leaflet on the kitchen table. "You can't buy groceries without these." She smiled nervously as she held out the booklet of ration stamps.

"No, I'd say you can't." Hans grinned.

Turning to the virtually empty refrigerator, Olivia opened it and looked inside, anxious for anything to keep her attention.

"Good news is," Hans said from behind her. "I don't think you'll be making any more meals for two after tonight."

"Oh?" Olivia questioned; her gaze locked on the half-empty bottle of milk on the refrigerator's top shelf.

"That is..." Hans said, hesitating to take a step towards her. "If

33

THE SECRET COURIER

you think I'm well enough to leave."

Olivia took a glimpse at Hans from the corner of her eye. He wore a white cotton t-shirt with his uniform's green slacks, but Olivia hadn't been able to completely remove the blood, even after numerous washing.

She spun around to get a better look at him. His cheeks, which had been ghost white for about two weeks, had returned to their normal hue. His blue eyes seemed to shine in ways they hadn't previously. He was attractive. There was no denying it. Olivia pushed the memories aside, her cheeks blushing a faint shade of pink.

"You certainly look as though you're feeling better," she said. Turning her attention to the cabinet, she removed the flour container from its shelf.

"I am," Hans said, barely a few steps away from her. Milla gulped and turned around to face him.

"Well, I'm sure you have important things waiting for you, so as far as I'm concerned you've got a clean bill of health." Olivia smiled at him, despite the fact that his look made her stomach spin.

"Wonderful," Hans said, matching her grin. Olivia nodded and returned her attention to the flour container on the counter.

THE SECRET COURIER

"When do you think you'll be leaving?" She inquired nonchalantly, putting one cup of flour into a big mixing basin.

"First thing in the morning, I suppose," Hans said with a tinge of regret in his tone. He leaned on the other counter and watched Olivia work.

"I wouldn't want to overstay my welcome, of course," he said with a chuckle.

"I don't think being shot and almost dying counts as 'overstaying your welcome'," she said.

Hans chucked. "Touché."

5

CHAPTER FIVE

Olivia took a quick breath in, the frigid winter air filling her lungs. She had just started her new work. She would be Gunther Sinclair's personal assistant, overseeing the German War Office in Holland. Her true mission would be to spy on the German official and his equivalents, relaying all she heard and saw to the Winslows, who would then report back to the British SIS.

Olivia climbed up the stone stairs of the massive brick structure that used to house Den Haag's City Hall but no longer did. Following the invasion, the Germans seized it as their own and used it as a hub for their war effort. She opened the front door with a trembling hand.

As she entered the room, a blast of heated air burnt her cheeks. She gazed about, taking in all she saw. Women sat at workstations, furiously typing away at their typewriters, while men in green uniforms bustled throughout the room, sometimes stopping at a desk to pick up a pile of documents or converse with the receptionist who had typed them.

"Name?" A voice rang out. Olivia's gaze shifted to the left, where she saw a small, slim guy with black hair brushed to one side.

"Well?" The guy looked up from his papers at her eagerly.

"Oh, uh," Olivia faltered, realizing the guy was addressing her.

"Olivia. Olivia Carter." The guy looked down, examining the paper in his hands, before checking down what Olivia believed was her name.

"Follow me," muttered the guy, walking away without looking at Olivia. Her heels clicked on the wooden floor as she ran after him.

"This is your workstation," the guy stated, halting in front of a little brown desk with a black typewriter on top of it.

"Of course, the typewriter is portable, given that you'll need to scribe during meetings. Its carrying case is located in the bottom drawer. The guy gave a tentative nudge towards it.

THE SECRET COURIER

"Now, Mr. Sinclair's morning meeting starts at 9 am sharp, you are to be there at 8:30."

The guy went on, putting another checkmark on his notepad.

"You will accompany Mr. Sinclair to any other meetings he requests. You are not permitted to talk at these sessions. You are not to worry Mr. Sinclair. You may contact me with any questions you may have.

"And you are?" Olivia enquired. His eyes squinted as he glanced up from his page. "Sir." Olivia spoke innocently.

"Franklin," he said, "but you can call me Mr. Mills." He turned and began to walk away. "Oh, by the way," Mr. Mills said over his shoulder, "Ms. Carter, that 9 a.m. meeting begins in five minutes."

Olivia let go of her purse and crouched down, opening her desk's bottom drawer. After placing the carrying case on her desk, she shoved the typewriter inside and began walking down the hall to the meeting room. If she was fortunate, Mr. Sinclair didn't start his meetings too early.

She shoved open the thick oak door, coming to a halt when she noticed the room was now crowded with several dozen uniformed men, all of whom had their gaze fixed on her. She looked around uneasily, her tummy doing a summersault as her

THE SECRET COURIER

eyes locked with a familiar blue pair.

"Ah, you must be the new typist," Olivia averted her gaze as she heard a voice shout from across the room. The guy at the head of the table had spoken.

"Come take a seat, we've only just began."

Olivia gulped hard, trying not to look at Hans, despite the fact that she could feel him digging holes into her as she moved across the room to sit beside Mr. Sinclair.

"Alright gentlemen," he said, "I'd like to start off by welcoming Hans Friedrich to our office."

Olivia bit her cheek, seeing Hans smirk and wave lazily across the room out of the corner of her eye.

"You see, the boys back in Berlin feel the office could use a little extra security following the attack we had last month," Sinclair went on to say. "It seems that our small Dutch pals attempted to outdo us once again. Fortunately, Mr. Friedrich arrived in one piece, although with a few gunshot wounds. The room laughed together.

"It's an honor to have you with us." Mr. Sinclair nodded towards Hans, who reciprocated.

Olivia kept her eyes fixed on the keys of her typewriter during the remainder of the meeting, which seemed to last forever. Olivia rose up and ran out of the room as the meeting finished.

39

THE SECRET COURIER

She'd been in the restroom for about 10 minutes, pondering her next steps.

When Hans departed three days ago, she believed he went north or possibly west to the front lines.

She had no idea his final destination was Den Haag all along.

She picked up her typewriter case and stepped out of the restroom, deciding that her only choice was to return and face whatever came her way. She sat down with her suitcase on her desk and began unpacking her belongings.

She caught Hans's stare out of the corner of her eye. He approached her, politely excusing himself from the group of guys he had been conversing with. Olivia clinched her teeth, battling the bad sensation that had arisen in her gut.

"Hello..." Hans said after reaching her desk. "Ms. Carter." Olivia glanced up as if she hadn't spotted him.

"I was surprised to see you this morning."

"I could say the same," Olivia said coolly, smiling sweetly at him.

"You didn't think to mention that you work for the German War Office?" Hans questioned, lifting an eyebrow.

"Well, today is my first day," Olivia said.

"Fair enough," Hans said smirking.

"Mr. Friedrich, do you two know each other?" Mr. Mills had

40

approached, his gaze darting between the two of them.

"Actually," Hans explained.

"We don't," Olivia interrupted.

Mr. Mills's gaze furrowed as he returned to Hans.

"Mr. Friedrich, may I remind you that fraternizing at one's workplace is typically frowned upon," he says.

"Even if you are a captain..." he said with a sneer.

"Noted," Hans said, a sneer spreading over his lips, "Franklin."

Mr. Mills glared, but said nothing. Hans leaned on her desk and returned his gaze to her. "So, we don't know each other?" He inquired, gently lifting his eyebrows. Olivia looked around the room, making certain that no one was listening in.

"Look," she said at that point, "I'd rather no one knew the circumstances of how we first met." She glanced up at Hans, who seemed puzzled. "I'd rather do without the attention," she said, attempting to make him understand.

"You would be a hero if you saved the life of a German commander... Why wouldn't you want the attention?"

"Because I'm no hero," Olivia said. "I just did what any decent person would've done."

6

CHAPTER SIX

Olivia strolled along the sidewalk, her scarf securely around her neck, while snowflakes dropped from the sky and melted as soon as they struck the ground. It had been snowing on and off for about a week, but Den Haag would not see its first real snowfall for nearly a month.

Olivia fled the office as soon as Mr. Mills fired her. She had left by turning down the familiar street she was presently on. The roadway that leads to Winslow's home. Olivia opened the wrought iron gate and knocked on the front door. It finally opened, showing an astonished Cecilia.

"Olivia, why are you here? Our next meeting is not scheduled until next Tuesday. Is not it?" Cecilia remarked, stepping aside to let Olivia enter.

"It isn't," Olivia responded as she entered. "But I thought there was something you should know." Cecilia raised her eyebrows in alarm.

"Sit down, and I'll get Harold," she said, walking down the hall. Olivia approached the couch and took a seat. Harold walked into the room after a little pause, followed by Cecilia.

"What's happened?" Harold inquired; his look as anxious as Cecilia's.

"That officer I saved?" Olivia started, opting to cut to the chase. "He works at the War Office. He is now in charge of security. Apparently, the Reich believes the city needs more following Sinclair's assassination attempt last month."

Harold gave Cecilia a knowing glance.

"Olivia, what exactly will he be doing?" Catharine inquired.

"Sinclair did not really say anything. Just that he'd be in charge of security," Olivia said. The Winslows shared a second glance.

"What?" Olivia inquired as she looked at the two of them.

"I want you to avoid this man," Harold said, his tone more serious than normal.

"Why?"

THE SECRET COURIER

"Because ... I don't think this officer is just an officer."

Olivia's face creased in puzzlement, but Harold persisted.

"If I had to guess, the Germans think the Resistance assisted in the preparation of last month's murder attempt. Who better to ask for aid than someone on the inside?"

"So, they think there's a mole?"

Harold indicated with a nod.

"Now this officer turns up and is appointed head of security? There is something missing from the story."

Olivia said, "What exactly are you saying?"

"I'm saying, stay away from Captain Friedrich... I don't believe he's come to serve as the general's glorified bodyguard.

Olivia glanced from Harold to Cecilia, then back again.

"You think he's here-,"

"To catch you," Harold cut in to complete her query.

7

CHAPTER SEVEN

Olivia sat alone in the breakroom, with a half-finished sandwich and a cold cup of coffee on the table in front of her. She had taken her lunch break about thirty minutes ago, despite the fact that she was not hungry, opting to utilize the time to catch up on her reading.

She turned over the pages of her book, putting the cup of coffee to her lips absentmindedly. She grimaced when the chilly liquid entered her mouth. Swallowing hard, she set the cup back down with a grimace. A chuckle came from across the room. Olivia glanced up and saw Hans standing at the entrance, leaning against the frame.

THE SECRET COURIER

"Not a coffee drinker?" he inquired, coming inside.

"Not when it's cold," Olivia said with a nice grin.

"Ah..." Hans grinned and leaned himself against the table. "Are you a Dickens fan?" he said, gesturing to the book she was holding. Olivia looked down at the copy of Bleak House she had been reading.

"I've always liked the classics," she shrugged, dog-earing the page before shutting the book and rising.

"Where are you going?"

"I should probably be getting back to work," Olivia said, taking her leftovers and putting them away. A hand wrapped around hers, tugging her backwards. Olivia glanced down to see Hans's hand grasping hers.

"There's something I've been wanting to ask you," He started, his hand still linked with hers.

"I never got the chance to thank you properly for saving my life."

"That's not necessary," Olivia said, removing her hand from his.

"I disagree," He continued ignoring Olivia's interjection.

"So ... I'd like to take you out to dinner."

Olivia took a big breath. "Mr. Friedrich..."

"Hans," he said, "call me Hans."

"Hans," Olivia said again,

"I'm not sure that would be such a good idea."

"Why not?"

"I- I mean, we... work together," Olivia stuttered, blushing.

"I just don't think it would be a good idea. I wouldn't want to get in trouble."

"With Franklin?" Hans laughed, a grin emerging at the corners of his lips. "He's just a private who takes his job a bit too serious."

"He could still fire me," Olivia said.

"No, he can't."

"And how do you know that?" Olivia inquired, raising an eyebrow.

"Because you haven't even been here a month and you've managed to impress General Sinclair. He likes you - and he's not a man easily won over," Hans said with a wide-eyed smile.

"Well-" Olivia started.

"And," Hans added, disregarding her argument, "you've managed to evade me every time I've intended to ask you out."

"Well - I..." Olivia began, turning bright crimson.

"It's dinner, not a marriage proposal," Hans said, crossing his arms and leaned against the wall.

Olivia bit her cheek, attempting to stifle the grin that tried to form on her lips. "Just dinner?" she inquired, raising one

THE SECRET COURIER

eyebrow.

"Just dinner," Hans said. Olivia hesitated, considering his offer. "You can pick me up on Saturday at 7:30," she eventually answered, taking her book from the table and headed to the door.

"Is that a Yes?" Hans yelled from behind.

"Don't be late," Olivia said, leaving Hans standing alone, a smile on his face.

***

"Let me get this straight... You're considering going on a date with a German officer?" Harold scoffed.

Olivia had been to the Winslow's home that evening for their planned Saturday meeting, and she had been sitting there for about an hour, listening to Harold berate her.

"If you would just listen to what I'm trying to tell you," Olivia cut in for what seemed like the fifteenth time. "And for the last time, I'm not thinking about it, I've already said yes."

"Harold, let us just hear her out, okay?" Cecilia spoke. She had been sitting there but hadn't said anything the whole time, though Olivia guessed she would've had something to say if she could get a word in edgewise around Harold.

48

THE SECRET COURIER

"Olivia, you must've had a solid reason for accepting this offer, so what is it?" Cecilia continued, staring eagerly at Olivia.

Olivia took in a big breath.

"I've been trying to avoid him, as you suggested," Olivia glanced in Harold's direction, and he emitted a low grumble, though he made no move to stop her this time.

"But he's been extremely persistent, and, for some reason, Mr. Friedrich has taken a shine to me... So, I decided, why not utilize it to our advantage?" Cecilia and Harold looked at her, a puzzled look on both of their faces.

"He likes me..." Olivia pushed on, "What better way to get information than from someone who wouldn't hesitate to give it to me."

"No," Harold interrupted, his tone stern and serious. "This concept of yours... What you are proposing... The most experienced representatives... People who have dedicated their lives to training... Even they can't accomplish their job perfectly every time."

"Olivia, he's correct," Cecilia said. "What you're trying to do requires more than simply conveying facts. It takes all you've got. Your feelings... Your sentiments. All of these factors might easily get engaged in a position like this. And it might affect your

THE SECRET COURIER

judgment before you know it. Can you confidently declare that you will not develop emotions for this man? That you can entirely disconnect yourself? Because if you can't..." Cecilia's voice drifted off.

"Because if you don't, you'll be murdered..." Harold cut in, "Or worse." Olivia glanced at the two of them; Harold's attitude was harsh, as it often was, but Cecilia was worried.

"You two don't think I've thought about all of this," Olivia said. "I know what I'm getting myself into. "And what about the dangers? I've seen directly what the Germans do to spies. Or have the two of you forgotten that I saw my father and brother receive a gunshot to the head?" She said forcefully. Cecilia and Harold exchanged glances.

"Have you made up your mind?"" Cecilia inquired, sighing.

"Yes," Olivia said forcefully.

"If you're doing this, you must send word after every interaction the two of you have. "I want updates on everything," Harold said, rising from his seat. Olivia nodded. Harold heaved an annoyed sigh. "Now, I'm going to have a tall glass of scotch." With that, Harold exited the room, retreating down the hall.

Cecilia rose from her seat, and Olivia followed suit. When they approached the door, Olivia twisted the knob, intending to

50

THE SECRET COURIER

open it, but Cecilia's hand grabbed hers.

"Be careful," Cecilia said, her hand clutching Olivia's.

"I will," Olivia said, putting her other hand on top of Cecilia's. "I can do this."

"I know you can."

8

CHAPTER EIGHT

Olivia walked along the sidewalk. Her visit with the Winslows had gone just as she expected. Harold was upset with her proposition, lecturing her on how silly and hazardous it was. Olivia had not anticipated Cecilia's answer, however. She had seemed agreeable to the notion. Concerned, definitely, but confident in Olivia's talents.

If Olivia was honest, the whole scheme made her uneasy. She was prepared to let an officer from the German army to take her to supper... She was not only Jewish, but also a spy for the 'enemy.' The Winslows had been correct to doubt her sanity. To

THE SECRET COURIER

be honest, she was questioning it as well.

A burst of chilly air sent shivers down her spine, so Olivia pulled her wool coat firmly about her, pulling up the collar to block the breeze. It was late, and the sun had long since vanished behind the city's skyline. She needed to return to her residence and prepare before Hans came.

Olivia went into a nearby alley after seeing a group of guys crowded on the pavement in front of her. She didn't want to attract unwanted attention to herself, particularly in this area. Suddenly, she was stopped by a towering figure in front of her. Taking a step back, her gaze rested on a German soldier.

"Oh, my apologies," she murmured quickly, removing her gaze from the tall guy.

"Not a problem at all," The guy talked slowly, his German accent heavy, and looked Olivia up and down. She gave the guy a brief nod before trying to sidestep him, but he moved in front of her, obstructing her route once again.

"You know ... a young woman like yourself shouldn't be walking alone at night," The guy started by taking a step towards her. "Why don't you let me escort you home?"

Olivia could smell the booze on his breath from where she stood, indicating that he had spent the evening in the tavern down the

53

THE SECRET COURIER

street.

"That's fine," Olivia answered, sidestepping the guy again.

"I think I can mana-" She was stopped by a hand clutching her arm, stopping her from moving forward.

Her gaze moved up to the person who held the hand. The soldier was glowering at her, his grasp tightening around her arm as their gazes met.

"I insist," he said bluntly.

"And I said," she continued, pulling her arm from his grip. "No." Olivia felt her back strike the alley wall in an instant, sending a piercing agony through her and leading her to drop her handbag to the ground. The guy was inches from her face, his breath heavy with booze, and his fingers gripped her neck.

"I think we need to learn some manners," the guy muttered to her ear. She raised her hands in protest, attempting to wrench the guy away from her, but he caught her wrists and pulled them over her head with one hand.

"Get off me! ... Help!" Olivia wept, hoping desperately that someone, anybody, would come to her assistance. Cold metal brushed on her flesh, stifling her screams. She raised her eyes to face her assailant.

THE SECRET COURIER

"What are you planning to do? "Kill me?" she questioned, a surge of defiance racing through her. The guy chuckled.

"I'll do whatever pleases me, sweetheart," he said, pressing the rough edge of his blade on her face. Olivia's jaw tightened and she pressed her eyes shut, choking back the terror that was eating her insides.

"That's much better," the guy remarked, releasing her wrists from his grip and running them down the length of her body. "Now be a good little girl."

This was not occurring... Olivia inhaled deeply as the man's lips touched her neck. The guy mistook it for pleasure and grinned against her flesh. "You like that?"

She twisted her head with distaste. She opened her eyes and saw the man's hand braced against the wall, knife in palm. He was no longer holding it to her neck, too preoccupied with wet kisses over the spot where the blade had been. Now was her moment; if she could only get to the street, that could be enough. Surely, someone would see her, hear her calls for aid, and respond.

Olivia swallowed and drove her knee up, firmly into the man's crotch. With a grunt, he let her go, bracing himself against the wall in anguish. She made a dash for it, only to be dragged back

THE SECRET COURIER

by her hair. The guy reached for her neck but grabbed the gold chain from her locket instead. It broke from around her neck, causing her to yell in agony as her body landed with a thud.

He was on top of her before she could blink, and he was furious. His eyes flashed with rage as he grabbed her by the neck again.

His nostrils flared as he peered down at her, tightening his hold around her neck till she could scarcely breathe. She grasped his hand, anxiously attempting to tear it from her. He had peeled aside her coat, leaving a path of sloppy kisses from her chest to her cleavage.

She clenched her eyes tight, attempting to think straight despite the terror that was running through her veins. She needed to go... escape. But how? She opened her eyes with a start. Her handbag! Her gun was inside her backpack! Glancing from side to side, she saw it a few feet distant from where she lay. She extended her arm and desperately searched for it. It was barely inches from her fingers.

She wiggled under him, attempting to make her way to the bag. The guy tightened his grasp on her neck, but did not glance up. He had slid his hand inside her dress and was now violently attempting to pull down her panties.

She stretched out again, this time gripping the bag's leather strap.

THE SECRET COURIER

Pulling it closer, she put her hand inside and searched for her revolver. Her palm grasping her neck had tightened to the point that she could see stars, but she had finally found what she was looking for. She quickly drew out the revolver and pushed it on the man's chest. She fired a single shot without hesitation, causing the soldier to yell and collapse on top of her.

Olivia coughed, drawing breath into her oxygen-deprived lungs. She scrambled furiously out from behind her attacker's dead corpse, dropping the pistol. Scooting backward, she placed her back against the wall, startled by what she had done. She gazed down at her bloodied clothing and hands, her breath caught in her throat. She needed to go right now. She snatched her coat from the ground and quickly put it on. She grabbed her rifle and hid it in her backpack before rushing into the alleyway.

***

Olivia slammed the door behind her. She raced to the bathroom, turning on the faucet in a panic. Placing her hands under the stream, she scrubbed them furiously, the water becoming crimson. She slammed her hands on the sink basin and glanced in the mirror. A stifled sob escaped her lips, and she started to weep. She turned and slid down the door, tears flowing down her face and more cries coming from her lips. She had slain the guy without thinking twice. She held her knees to her body, swaying back and forth as she cried.

Finally, after what seemed like hours, the weeping stopped. She braced herself against the sink and went for the door, trekking down the hall to her bedroom.

She unbuttoned the front of her dress and discarded it in a corner. She unlocked her closet and took out a light blue outfit. She slipped it over her head and looked at her reflection in the floor-length mirror.

Her legs and arms were bruised and wounded from hitting the pavement. She breathed loudly, rubbing her hands through her ratted hair to straighten it down.

Olivia was startled when she heard a knock on the door. Hans... she had forgotten about their intentions in the aftermath of all that had transpired. She couldn't watch him like this, especially after what she'd done. She slipped on her robe and approached the front door, just in time to hear another knock.

"Olivia, it's Hans," a voice said from the other side of the door. Olivia gulped.

"I don't think I can go out tonight," she said nervously. "I'm not feeling well."

"Are you okay?" Hans phoned back. When she did not respond, he knocked again. "Olivia ..."

THE SECRET COURIER

"I'm fine," she gasped out.

"Olivia, open the door."

"Just go, please!" She called back, forcing her eyes tight, tears threatening to flow again.

"Olivia, open the door, or I will," Hans said, his voice becoming increasingly frantic. Olivia shook her head and ran a palm over her face, frustrated. Wrapping her robe snugly about her body, she breathed and pulled herself up to her full height. She grabbed the doorknob and turned it, and the door clicked open. Hans stood before her; his face wrinkled with anxiety.

"Are you okay?" He inquired, his gaze going down her body, pausing abruptly at the bruises and wounds on her forearms.

"I'm fine," she said, pulling the sleeves of her robe down and crossing her arms over her chest.

"No, you're not ..." He shakes his head. Taking a step towards her, he grabbed her arms and pulled them away from her. She winced in agony, and his brow wrinkled deeper.

"What happened?" He questioned, tugging her sleeves up and turning her arms over in his hands to study them more closely.

"Nothing," she muttered, ripping her arms free of his grip. "Nothing happened." She turned and went a few steps, wrapping her arms about her core again.

THE SECRET COURIER

"Olivia ..." Hans started, but then trailed off, watching her go away. He followed her farther into the room, and she gulped hard, her heart racing out of her chest.

"Did someone hurt you?" He asked after a lengthy gap.

She glanced up at him, avoiding her gaze as it caught on his.

She clinched her teeth and scrunched up her face to avoid crying. He would not watch her weep. If it were the last thing she did, she would force herself not to weep. She silently nodded her head. His jaw tightened briefly before his face relaxed.

"What happened?"

"Someone attacked me," Olivia said, unwilling to look at him. "On my way home from town."

"Who was it?" Hans inquired, anchored to his spot. She shrugged her shoulders.

"I don't know," she lied. "He assaulted me from behind and shoved me to the ground. I've never seen his face."

"Did he..." Hans started, trailing off as if he had lost the courage to continue the inquiry. Olivia gazed at him, perplexed, before realizing what was going on.

"No," she said immediately, her cheeks burning. "No. He didn't.

I heard voices approaching us, which must have startled him since he raced in the other direction."

"You need to report it, I can -" Hans started.

"No," Olivia stopped him off. "I don't want to report it."

"Olivia..." Hans put his hands on her shoulders and carefully seated her on a kitchen chair before taking a seat next her.

"You should report this. They can find the individual who did this and arrest him."

"No," Olivia said. "I don't want anyone knowing."

"It's nothing to be ashamed of Mi-"

"I know it's not," Olivia cut in humiliation. "It's just, if the men in the office knew..." She trailed off, trying to think of an explanation. "If they'd heard what occurred. They would not respect me."

"Yes, they would," Hans insisted.

"No, they won't... They would pity me, just as you are doing now." She cut him off. "It's hard enough to be the lone woman at those meetings. If they knew what happened tonight, those men would never take me seriously."

Hans nodded and studied her for a bit before standing up and walking into the kitchen without saying anything.

"What are you doing?" She inquired, observing him as he

THE SECRET COURIER

opened the refrigerator.

"You're in no mood to go out tonight, so I suppose we'll just have dinner here," Hans said, opening the cabinets.

"You don't have to do this," Olivia said.

"I want to," Hans said genuinely, looking at her for a while before returning his attention to the cabinet. "Besides, I've been told I'm a very good cook."

9

CHAPTER NINE

"General Sinclair has you fetching his coffee now?"

Olivia glanced up from the stack of papers she had been delicately balancing a coffee cup on, her gaze meeting Hans's blue ones.

"Well," she shrugged, heaving her typewriter case onto her desk before putting the cup down, taking care not to spill any of the contents.

"I am his secretary." She gathered the documents she had been carrying and laid them flat against the surface, putting them inside a blue file folder she had grabbed from her desk drawer.

THE SECRET COURIER

"Hey," Hans said, touching her forearm and whispered gently so no one could hear. "How are you doing?"

"I'm..." She hesitated, resisting the unpleasant thoughts she had been trying to ignore. "Getting on." It had been a little more than a week after her encounter with the German soldier, and despite the fact that she and Hans had attended several meetings and seen one other around the workplace, neither had discussed what had happened that night. Olivia had instead immersed herself into her job, wishing with every fiber of her existence that the memories would cease.

"Despite everything that happened the other night, I really enjoyed spending the evening with you," he added, gently squeezing her arm before releasing it.

"I enjoyed your company as well," she answered, smiling slightly.

"Seeing as we have yet to go on a proper date, I was wondering if you'd let me take you out this Friday night?" He went on, leaning himself up against her desk, his anxious look giving way to a cheeky chuckle.

"I thought your taking me out to dinner was just repayment for saving your life?" She questioned, arching her brow.

"It was..." He answered, his smirk spreading. "I don't think I'm done returning the favor just yet though."

"Well, if you're that insistent on it," she said, attempting to hide a grin. "You can pick me up at 6:30."

"It's a date," Hans said, grinning. Olivia nodded, offering him a little grin before taking her typewriter and folder.

"Olivia!" Hans yelled after she had moved a few steps. "I think you're forgetting something," He replied, indicating to the coffee cup remaining on her desk.

"Oh," she reddened, eagerly grabbing the cup with her free hand.

"See you in there," he grinned and winked at her.

"See you," she said, reciprocating his grin.

Olivia walked down the hallway, her shoes tapping on the floor. She nudged the conference room door with her hip and pushed it open, displaying General Sinclair sat at the head of the large table, poring over a stack of documents, as he did every morning at 8:30. Olivia moved across the room without saying anything, placing the cup on General Sinclair's seat.

"Oh, thank you, Ms. Carter," he said, peering up from his wire-rimmed spectacles briefly before returning to his reading.

"Here are the minutes from yesterday's meeting," Olivia said, laying the blue folder next to the coffee cup. "I thought you might like to give them a once over before I file them away."

"Oh yes," he said, gazing back in her way. "Thank you."

THE SECRET COURIER

"Of course," she said, setting her typewriter in her normal position at the table.

"What's this?" General Sinclair inquired as she was unzipping her case. Olivia turned and watched as he picked up the piece of paper she had inadvertently placed on the folder.

"Oh," she stuttered. "It is nothing. This is just a list I made for myself. It sets forth the agenda for each meeting... Helps me stay on track while I'm entering the minutes."

"I like it," he said after perusing the page. "How quickly could you make twenty copies?"

"Twe-twenty copies?" Olivia wrinkled her head in perplexity.

"One for you and me, of course, as well as the men," he said matter-of-factly.

"These briefings might use some organization, and I believe this short list of yours will suffice. A firm routine for each morning would be ideal, something the guys could adhere to."

"Oh," she said, her cheeks blushing a pale pink.

"That is, if you'd be willing to share," he said, taking his glasses and placing them on the table, a slight grin curling his lips.

"Of course, sir," she said, receiving the document from him as he handed it out.

Olivia opened the conference room door, her heels clicking

THE SECRET COURIER

even faster than before, and raced to the copy room, her typewriter in tow.

She had less than 30 minutes to create a stencil and print 20 copies before to the meeting. She heaved her typewriter onto the copy room desk, inserted a piece of waxed paper into the ribbon, and began typing. After successfully copying the agenda, she took it out and gave it a quick once over before inserting it into the mimeograph. She turned the handle around and started making copies. She raced back down the corridor to the briefing room, clutching the documents and her typewriter.

"Ah, Ms. Carter," General Sinclair said as she rushed through the door, all eyes on her. "Were you able to get those duplicates finished?"

"Yes, sir," she said.

"If you don't mind, I'll pass them around." He smiled politely.

"Of course," she said, nodding. She strolled around the room, balancing her typewriter on her hip, handing a sheet to each of the guys, being cautious not to make eye contact with Hans when she reached his spot at the table for fear of blushing. After distributing the last copy, she returned to her accustomed place alongside General Sinclair.

"Now," the general clasped his hands together, "if you'd all refer to your agendas, which Ms. Carter had kindly drawn up for us, let's get started."

"Shultz," he said, directing his attention to a lanky, blonde-haired guy sitting at the end of the table.

"What word do you have from Berlin?"

"The Red Army has launched a counterattack in Stalingrad, sir," Shultz stated in answer. "The Sixth Army has been instructed to maintain their position and await reinforcements."

"Any word on casualties?"

"80,000 of our troops - 150,000 of theirs."

"What is being done to offer reinforcement?" General Sinclair furrowed his brow slightly, but otherwise seemed unconcerned.

"As we speak, two distinct infantry units are marching toward Stalingrad, and supplies are being collected to be carried back to Berlin and flown into the city to offer meals to the surviving men besieged there."

"Lieutenant Hayesn," General Sinclair said, referring to a brown-haired guy with a little larger physique than Shultz. He didn't seem much older than her.

"I want labor camps to work extra shifts to meet demand. We will not lose Stalingrad due to insufficient supplies."

"Of course, sir," The Lieutenant spoke a bit too excitedly, as if the prospect of pushing prisoners to labor in even harder

THE SECRET COURIER

circumstances made him extremely happy.

***

The remainder of the conference had passed in a languid drawl. Olivia listened closely, transcribing everything that was said as each bullet item on the agenda was covered, taking special attention to anything that may be relevant to the Winslows and the British SIS. Finally, once General Sinclair had left the room, Olivia collected her belongings and dropped them down at her desk before eating lunch.

She was now sat in the break room, with her normal coffee cup and sandwich in front of her, her nose buried deep in a book, as she usually did at this hour.

"Hello," a deep voice said beside her. She glanced up and saw Lieutenant Hayesn's familiar face.

"Hello, Lieutenant Hayesn," she said, looked up from her book briefly.

"So you know who I am?" He grinned.

"You spoke at this morning's meeting," she said simply. "You're the labor camp liaison."

"Well, since we seem to be acquainted," he sat alongside her, "I suppose you can call me Matthew."

She returned her focus to her book, smiling politely.

69

THE SECRET COURIER

"You know," he said nonchalantly. "Every time I see you in here, you've got a book in your hand."

"I like to read," she shrugged, dog-earing the page, figuring she wouldn't be getting anything done for the remainder of the lunch hour. "And between all the meetings and briefings, lunch is one of the only times I get to."

"Maybe you should take a vacation from your reading. Say, this Friday night?" He inquired, but it came across more as a command than a question.

"Oh," Olivia murmured, surprised by his forwardness. "I, um ... actually have plans this Friday."

"Some other time then," he answered, clearly unconcerned with her rejection.

"I should get back to work," she responded, swiftly grabbing her belongings. Without saying anything further, she rose up and moved toward the door, slipping out before he could complain.

10

CHAPTER TEN

"So, Hitler's marching his men to Stalingrad?" Harold inquired, reclining back in the armchair he had seated himself in at the start of their encounter.

Olivia had come directly to the Winslows' house after work, as she had done every Friday since, for their weekly meeting, and had begun to pass along the plans for Stalingrad she had been hearing about since earlier that week.

"That seems to be the case." She nodded. "The Reich is gathering supplies up and flying it out of Berlin too... To aid the men still trapped there."

THE SECRET COURIER

"I knew the Germans would be too proud to give up a stronghold like Stalingrad..." Harold growled and took a gulp from his Scotch glass.

"Losing that territory would be a huge blow to the Russians, and those bastards know it."

"Which is why they can't hold it," Cecilia said, her forehead pinched in concentration, as it often did during their sessions.

"Olivia, you should learn more about the transports taking place in Berlin. What materials they're accumulating... dates and times they want to fly the cargo out."

"She's right," Harold acknowledged. "If the allies can stop the shipments before they get to the city, then the Germans stranded in Stalingrad won't stand a bloody chance once winter really sets in."

"How are they planning on gathering that large a volume of supplies?" Cecilia pushed.

"They've already turned the bulk of their civilian enterprises into military facilities. Their people are practically starving."

"I think they plan to use the labor camps..." Olivia trailed off, her stomach churning as she thought about it.

"Of course they are..." Cecilia sneered. "Use the dispensable prisoners to supply your war effort."

THE SECRET COURIER

"Is this Captain Friedrich still taking you out tonight?" Harold asked.

"Yes," Olivia said, nodding.

"Good," he said, taking another draw from his glass.

"Keep it casual, nothing too serious, and see what you can get from him. The chief of security knows when and where these shipments will take place.

***

"Where are we going?" Olivia asked, hiding her eyes with her palms. She left the Winslows with barely enough time to go home and refresh herself before Hans came to pick her up for their date.

"You'll see," Hans said, the smile on his face clear in his tone.

"I'm not too keen on surprises," she answered, but the corners of her lips had curled up into a faint grin at the eagerness in his voice.

"We're almost..." Hans trailed off, the vehicle coming to a gradual halt before he shifted the brakes and shut off the engine. "So here we are. You can open your eyes."

Putting her hands down, she gazed about, her gaze resting on the bright lights of a marquee.

"We're going to the theatre?" She inquired, shifting her attention to Hans.

73

THE SECRET COURIER

"I thought it'd be fun," he smiled, getting out of the vehicle and heading around to the passenger side to open her door for her.

"Watching a propaganda film for two hours?" She inquired, raising a doubtful eyebrow.

"For your information, we'll be watching a classic tonight," Hans smirked, taking her hand and walking her inside.

***

"I think we need to work on your definition of a classic," Olivia said, a grin forming on the corners of her lips as they went down the sidewalk, her arm looping around Hans's.

"What are you talking about?" He inquired with faux incredulity. "King Kong is a cinematic masterpiece."

"It was certainly something," she laughed. "Besides, how were we able to view it? I thought it was banned in Germany before the war."

"Well..." Hans smirked. "We're not in Germany now, are we?"

"Fair enough," Olivia smiled. "Where to now?"

"There's a little cafe down the street-," he said.

"Oh, thank goodness ... I'm starved!" She interrupted, her smile broadening at the mention of food. Except for the popcorn during the movie, she hadn't eaten anything since her customary sandwich and coffee at noon.

THE SECRET COURIER

They walked side by side to the café on the corner, where the server quickly seated them after seeing Hans's outfit.

"So, tell me about yourself," Hans said when they had received their beverages. "I feel like I hardly know anything about you," he said, gazing over the menu he was casually scanning.

"I believe I've already told you everything there is to know," she said, looking up from her own menu.

"Well, considering I had a hole in my abdomen and a high fever when you told me your life story, you'll have to forgive me for not remembering every word," he said with a chuckle.

"I suppose that's fair," she laughed. "What do you want to know?"

"Everything," he said simply, leaning over the table and waited carefully.

"Alright," she stopped for a bit, carefully considering which information were safe to give and which should be left out.

"I grew up in a home just outside of town with my parents, brother, and sister. We lived there until my mother died..." She hesitated, realizing that this was the first time she'd discussed her mother to Hans. "Typhoid fever," she said, as his brow wrinkled in anxiety.

"That's when my father moved us to the city. He said that he

THE SECRET COURIER

wanted to be closer to his practice... To be honest, I don't believe he could live there much longer... There are too many memories." She hesitated again, looking up at Hans, who had the same worried face as before. She cleared her throat awkwardly, recognizing that their talk had taken a negative turn.

"All three of us attended primary and secondary school in Den Haag. My brother went to university after graduating... He was in the process of applying to medical school before..." She drifted off, hoping not to bring up any more depressing issues than she had already.

"You and your sister never thought about going as well?" Hans asked, following her lead and moving on from the topic.

"I had thought about it," she said, nodding. "Then the war started and things ... Changed."

"I understand that all too well," Hans said, nodding.

"Grace, on the other hand," she grinned, considering the possibility of her sister entering college. "I don't think university was ever part of her plan."

"I'm sure if she's as sharp as you-," Hans started.

"Oh, she's exceptionally bright," She interrupted him. "However, the notion of sitting in a classroom never appealed to her... Even as we grew up. She'd rather fall in love and settle down in

THE SECRET COURIER

a large, gorgeous home with children," she giggled.

"And you wouldn't?" He grinned.

"I think the whole idea is... romantic," she said, smiling. "This sounds like something out of a book. But I have always sought more."

"More than being a wife and a mother?"

"Is it so impossible to believe a woman can be those things and, at the same time, something else entirely?"

"Not at all," Hans laughed.

"What's so funny?" She questioned, raising an eyebrow.

"Nothing," he smiled and shook his head. "You just remind me of my sister." His grin grew wider at the idea of her.

"Her name is Marie. She's sixteen and as driven as you. I recall when my brother and I enlisted, she pitched a tantrum when she realized she wouldn't be joining us..." He laughed.

"She was thirteen at the time. After I had been gone about a year," he said, his toothy smile spreading even more. "I got a letter from her. She stated the sole saving grace during the war was that our mother did not force her to complete school."

"It doesn't sound like learning which fork to use with dessert would excite her much," she said.

"Certainly not," Hans responded, chuckling.

THE SECRET COURIER

"So, if she's not attending finishing school, what is she doing?"

"Helping my parents run the store," Hans shrugged.

"I thought your father was an accountant?" She inquired, furrowing her brow.

"He is," he confirmed with a nod. "But dad also has a little business in town; he's had it since before I was born, inherited from my grandpa.

Mom is in charge of the front desk, while Dad is responsible for the books. I used to work there every afternoon after school, and we all did."

"Were you going to go back after you finished school?"

"That was the plan," Hans agreed. "The store would've eventually been mine."

"Would've?" She asked.

"I'm not so sure now," he said, leaning forward, his brow furrowing slightly as he looked down at his hands, which were tightly gripped on the table.

"I'd like to think I could go back after everything's said and done but war, it..." He drifted off, as if unable to find the appropriate words.

"Changes things," she said, seeking the right words for him.

He glanced up from his hands, his eyes finding her own. His

THE SECRET COURIER

light blue irises seemed to intensify somewhat, a piercing deep blue looking into her green before lightening at the sight of her. Her stomach flipped as she returned his look, doing cartwheels inside her belly with each passing second.

"So," she cleared her throat nervously, forcing down the butterflies that had started to appear in her chest. "What did you do for fun growing up?"

"Well," Hans said, clearing his throat as well. "I played a lot of football, especially when I was younger, but also while at university. What about you?"

"There wasn't much to do around here when I was growing up..." She drifted off, thinking about her upbringing. "I usually assisted my father at the clinic. We all did, but I believe I had the most fun of the three of us," she said, laughing. "It never really felt like work to me like it did to Grace and Maxwell."

"Still," Hans said. "There must've been something you did for fun?"

"Well, there was one thing," she hesitated, a faint grin forming on her lips.

"What?" He pushed, raising an eyebrow.

"Every year, after the first real snow, my father would take us to this lake outside of town and we would ice-skate," Her grin grew as thoughts of the lake returned to her mind. The ice in the

THE SECRET COURIER

winter light has a brilliant, almost transparent sheen... The sound of her skates flowing smoothly over the cool ice. She recalled everything as if it had occurred yesterday. A vision of simpler, brighter days is firmly etched in her mind.

"How long has it been since you've been?" Hans inquired, scrutinizing her attentively, as if he could sense the memory's bittersweetness.

"Oh, it's been years," she said, shrugging off the aching in her chest that the inquiry had caused. It had been the winter since Germany invaded Poland.

Despite the dread that came with being on the verge of war, her father insisted on continuing the annual custom. They had woken up early that December morning and arrived to the lake just after daybreak. Lacing up their skates, they had spent the whole day on the ice, ignoring all of the doubts and worry that the next year would undoubtedly bring as they skated through the fresh winter air. It had been the most amazing day, and one of the last she had ever enjoyed. The following three years had only given her anxiety and sorrow, with the recollection of such a wonderful moment exacerbating the nightmare whenever she thought about it. "War..." She trailed off as another ache shot through her chest.

"Changes things," Hans said, finally finding the words for her.

He reached across the table and squeezed her hands.

She offered him a little grin and returned his squeeze with her own. "Exactly."

11

CHAPTER ELEVEN

"Ms. Carter," Franklin Mills said, tapping the end of his pen on Olivia's desk impatiently.

"Have you finished those reports I asked you to do last week?"

"Oh," she faltered, looking up from her keyboard and into Mr. Mills's anxious eyes. Between drafting out the schedule for each morning's briefing and attending all of the additional meetings General Sinclair had recently held, she had entirely forgotten about the reports Mr. Mills had requested her to write up last week. She had no idea why he'd assigned her the assignment in the first place. She had had a sneaky impression he didn't like

THE SECRET COURIER

her from their first meeting, and that feeling only became stronger when he starting assigning her odd chores and duties that any other typist in the office could handle, just to pile them on top of the never-ending mountain of work she already had.

"Well?" Mr. Mills pushed, repeatedly pressing his pen on her desk.

"I'm sure they're here somewhere," she paused, pretending to seek for the completed reports behind a mound of papers.

"Surprise surprise," Mr. Mills said, taking up an olive-green folder from the pile and held it up with two fingers.

"Yet another assignment left unfinished," he said, opening the folder and scrolling through the original handwritten reports in a fake quest for her typed copy.

"I'm sorry, Mr. Mills," Olivia said, her cheeks warming crimson.

"I'll get to work on those right away," she said, though she wasn't sure how she'd find the time to complete those reports on top of everything else she had to accomplish.

"Is there a problem?" Hans's rich voice seemed nonchalant as he approached the two of them.

"It appears Ms. Carter is struggling to keep up with her workload," Mr. Mills replied, a delighted grin forming on the corners of his lips. Oh, why did he loathe her so much?

"I assigned these reports nearly a week ago, and they're still not

THE SECRET COURIER

finished," he said, tossing the folder onto her desk.

"Funny," Hans said, taking a pull from the cigarette in his palm, his brow wrinkled as if he were completely perplexed.

"Ms. Carter seems to be keeping up well with what General Sinclair expects of her. Speaking about," he said, tossing a new stack of paperwork onto her desk, flattening the one Mr. Mills had sat on. "I was going to bring you these... They are from meetings the General attended today. He asked if you could produce copies of each department's report for all the department heads."

"Of course," Olivia said, staring at the files closely. To her dismay, she had not been invited to attend any of the meetings scheduled for that afternoon. She suspected this since the General had been discussing extremely sensitive information, such as the locations and timings of supply shipments, which she badly needed to get.

"Ahem," Mr. Mills cleared his throat, clearly agitated by Hans's intrusion.

"Oh, my apologies," Hans murmured, raising the bottom edge of the files he had set on her desk and removing Mr. Mills's tiny, green one from behind them. "Here you go, Franklin," he

THE SECRET COURIER

replied, returning the file to Mr. Mills with an innocent smile, but his mouth twitched slightly as a smirk sought to pull up the corners of his lips.

"I'm assuming you can find someone else to finish these for you, since we can both agree these take precedence." he proceeded by patting the stack he had put there.

"I suppose I'll have to." Mr. Mills accepted the folder and returned to his office without saying anything further, but the frown on his face indicated that he was not pleased.

"I'd take a look at this one first," Hans remarked, his smile clearly visible as he tapped his finger on the file at the top of the pile. He gave her a short wink before turning around and returning to the corridor from whence he had come.

She tried not to grin as he walked away, passing through the door to his office. Turning her attention to the folders in front of her, she cautiously opened the top one, which had a little slip of paper on top of the reports General Sinclair intended for her to duplicate.

I need to see you again. I will pick you up on Saturday at 3 p.m. Dress warmly.

- Hans.

THE SECRET COURIER

She grinned to herself as she took one final look down the corridor, her gaze lingering on the door Hans had vanished behind.

Folding the paper, she put it into her pocket for safety before returning her attention to the papers on her desk. She started scanning each line methodically, trying not to think about what she and Hans were going to do on Saturday afternoon.

THE SECRET COURIER

12

CHAPTER TWELVEE

Olivia stood in front of the mirror, eyeing the blue sweater she had picked from her wardrobe, carefully fastening each button with shaky fingers.

She had been pacing around the house all morning, nervously anticipating Hans's arrival. She didn't understand why she felt so nervous. Perhaps it was the fact that she had failed to elicit any valuable information from Hans so far, or that the papers she had been ordered to copy earlier that week had yielded not a single piece of information for her to discuss the transports. She had thought the papers would have given her a hint... something to bring up lightly during their talk.

THE SECRET COURIER

However, the files contained no mention of the anticipated transfers to Berlin... Not a single reference of a time, date, or location.

Smoothing down the front of her sweater, she took one final look in the mirror before leaving the bedroom and entering the kitchen. She grabbed her red wool coat from the peg by the entrance and slid it on, buttoning it up. Hans had told her to dress warm, but no matter how hard she tried, she could not figure out what he had planned for the day.

She peeked behind the curtain and gazed out the window. A new layer of snow had fallen overnight and throughout the morning, with the harsh rays of the midday sun glinting off the white surface, making her eyes burn as they acclimated to the brightness. It was a gorgeous day, a welcome break from the chilly darkness that had enveloped the city throughout the previous month.

Her gaze wandered down the street as the sound of tires crunching through snow filled her ears, and she saw Hans's familiar, sleek gray vehicle approaching. She grabbed her hat and scarf from the hanger and put them on before picking up her bag from the kitchen table just in time to hear a tap on the

THE SECRET COURIER

door.

"Hello," she began as she opened the door, her gaze resting on Hans, who was dressed in ordinary clothing rather than his military wear. She saw the blue flannel button down he wore beneath his gray coat. As ludicrous as it was, she had been so used to his uniform that she had forgotten he may really possess ordinary clothing.

"I almost didn't recognize you," she laughed, pointing to his clothes.

"I'm off duty this weekend," He smiled, seizing her hand as they walked down the porch. "Besides, I didn't really think the uniform would be appropriate for what I have planned."

"What exactly do you have planned?" She inquired, stepping into the passenger seat of the vehicle after he had opened the door for her.

"It's a surprise," He grinned, shutting the door before she could object.

"You know I don't like surprises," she added after he had in from the opposite side and started the vehicle.

"I know," he said, his smile spreading wider. "It makes surprising you that much more fun."

"Uh-huh," she rolled her eyes, concealing a tiny grin on her lips.

THE SECRET COURIER

They started their voyage by pulling out of the driveway, the most of which was spent in small conversation, with the sound of snow crunching under the tires filling in the stillness.

"Where are we going?" Olivia inquired after they had drove for over 20 minutes.

"You'll see," Hans said, pulling off the main road onto a tiny dirt road that was still covered in snow from the morning and hadn't yet been plowed for driving. "We're nearly there."

"Are you sure you know where you're going?" She grinned, raising a skeptical eyebrow at him.

"Actually, I do," Hans said with a delighted smile, driving off the road into a little shoulder. Olivia glanced about; there was nothing but a wall of pine trees on each side of them, and the only bare area of earth was a little clearing to the right with an ice pond in the middle.

"Come on," Hans urged, shutting off the vehicle and opening the door.

She pulled the doorknob, opened the door, and slid out. Wrapping her scarf snugly over her neck, she turned back to face Hans, who was searching through the trunk for something.

"Um, Hans," she said, an instinctive knot growing in her chest as she realized, for the first time, that she was absolutely alone in

THE SECRET COURIER

the middle of nowhere, with a German officer she hardly knew. She tightened her grip on her bag as she made her way around to the rear of the vehicle, her gloved fingers pushing into the leather of her purse, feeling the firm indentation of the revolver within.

"I'm sure you're wondering what we're doing out here," Hans said, slamming the trunk with one hand as the other hid something behind his back.

"That story about going ice skating you told me on our last date," he said, tightening the tightness in her chest even more. Oh God... What if she had revealed too much? What if he had discovered her identity?

"I thought maybe you'd like to go again," he remarked, removing two pairs of ice skates from behind his back and smiling.

She let out a sigh of relief, the tension in her chest instantly releasing at the sight of the skates he had in his palm.

"I know this isn't the place you and your family used to go, but I asked around town and found this little spot," he said, gesturing to the clearing. "And I figured it would do just fine."

"It's perfect," she beamed, her heart racing with excitement rather than anxiety.

"Come on," He urged, holding out a hand for her to accept. Accepting it, they strolled hand in hand towards the pond,

THE SECRET COURIER

halting just short of its edge, where a big log lay on its side. After brushing off the snow, they sat down and took off their shoes.

"Where did you manage to find these?" She questioned, getting to her feet and gently balancing herself on the skate blades.

"I have my sources," he said coyly, continuing tightening his own laces. After he finished, he rose up, his knees trembling as he attempted to regain his equilibrium.

"Come on," she urged, turning to go to the edge of the ice. She pushed off, gently pressing her skate into the slick surface. Looking over her shoulder, she saw Hans, who was still standing apprehensively on the embankment. She turned on the toe of her skate and slid back in his way.

"What is it?" She inquired once she had approached him.

"I've..." He trailed off, a little sheepish grin pulling on the corners of his mouth. "Never actually been ice skating before."

"I'll teach you then," she grinned and extended her hand. "Come on," she laughed as he gave her a doubtful look.

"The trick is to keep a wide center of gravity," she said as he took her hand and went out onto the ice.

"Wide center of gravity," he repeated, as if he were receiving an instruction from a superior. "Got it."

"Now," she said, sinking the toe of her skate into the ice as Hans mimicked her every action. "Push off with your toe." They pushed off together, hands securely gripped, and forced themselves forward, Hans gripping Olivia's hand to keep himself upright.

"Good," she responded as he recovered his equilibrium. "Now, push off with the other foot." They went ahead, pushing off with the left foot first, then the right, until they had achieved significant momentum and speed. "You're doing it!" Olivia smiled, looking across at Hans, who was concentrating as they continued to glide over the ice.

"Okay, now let's turn," she remarked as they approached the edge of the pond. "Point your toe in and-," She was cut short as Hans's fingers dragged her backwards, his back hitting the ice with a crash as his feet slipped out from beneath him, pushing Olivia down onto her buttocks.

"Are you okay?" Hans inquired, wincing as he sat up, brushing the snow from his hair.

"I am fine... You look like you've seen better days," Olivia giggled, unable to contain her delight at his untidy appearance.

"Is something funny?" He inquired, raising an eyebrow as she assisted him to his feet.

"Just that you look like the abominable snowman," she snickered,

THE SECRET COURIER

wiping a coating of ice and snow off his coat's sleeves, which were coated in white powder.

"Well," he said, stooping down and pretending to brush his pants. "I'm glad I could be of amusement."

In an instant, he grasped her waist and dragged her into a snowdrift on the pond's edge.

"Oh my gosh!" Olivia gasped as she sat up, her coat and every other inch of her plastered in snow.

"Whoops," Hans shrugged, his lips curled into a playful grin. "I slipped again."

"Oh, you are so going to get it!" Olivia mocked at his pretended innocence. She grabbed a fistful of snow and tossed it at him, the white ball of powder shattering on his chest before he had time to react. Hans responded, grabbing snow in both hands and threw handfuls at her. Trying to avoid the snowballs being thrown at her, she got up, only to be dragged back down into the snowdrift by Hans.

"I think I won," he whispered, towering over her with his hands on each side of her head and supporting himself up.

"For now," she said, the tightness in her chest returning, this time to her stomach, as a surge of butterflies passed through her.

THE SECRET COURIER

He was hung over her, his face inches from hers. She looked up at him, suddenly becoming acutely conscious of their closeness. His eyes swept her face, looking for something, but she didn't know what. Despite the fact that her coat was wet in snow, her whole body felt heated, and her pulse was racing as he continued to stare down at her closely.

"I'd really like to kiss you," he added after a time, his gaze meeting hers. She gulped hard, fighting back the waves of tense anticipation that threatened to overwhelm her. Leaning down till their noses were almost touching, he looked into her eyes, his hot breath on her lips sending an uncontrollable shudder down her spine. "But only if you want me to."

"I want you to," she said breathlessly.

He paused for a while, looking down at her, before shutting his eyes and placing his lips on hers...

THE SECRET COURIER

13

CHAPTER THIRTEEN

Olivia opened her front door, untying and removing her snow-covered boots before walking inside. After the kiss, she and Hans skated a few more laps around the pond before returning home. She returned Hans's wool coat to him after wearing it for the rest of their time at the pond since hers had been drenched with snow.

"Sorry about your coat," he joked, taking his back and putting it on the coat rack. He kicked off his boots and set them alongside Olivia's before following her into the kitchen.

"It's okay," she said, opening a closet and removing a tin

THE SECRET COURIER

container off the shelf. "Would you like some tea?"

"Tea would be wonderful," he said, resting against the counter and watched her fill the kettle with water and place it on the fire. "I'm surprised they gave you the weekend off with these supply transports to Berlin happening so soon," She remarked as casually as she could, taking two teabags from the tin and returning it to the cabinet. Despite being disoriented by their kiss at the pond, she had not lost sight of her search for answers. She needed those transit dates and times if it was the last thing she ever did, and Hans was the only person who could provide her with that information.

"I suppose General Sinclair figured I could use a couple days since things are about to get even busier," he said with a smirk.

Olivia nodded, inserting a teabag into each of the cups she had retrieved from a shelf.

"How are they planning to get those supplies to Berlin?" She continued on nonchalantly. "Aren't they worried about Dutch Resistance or the Allies intercepting them?"

"That's certainly a concern," Hans said, taking the cup she offered him. "Moving the supplies by air would be ideal, but there is a high risk of those planes being shot down before they reach Berlin," he said, taking a drink of tea.

"Train would be the second fastest option, but Dutch Resistance

THE SECRET COURIER

know the supply routes too well so the risk of interception before the supplies makes it out of Holland would be too great."

"That leaves supply trucks," Olivia said, sipping from her cup.

Hans nodded, walked over to the kitchen table, pulled out a chair, and sat down. "Large cities like Munster and Hanover will be avoided, of course, because they are on the Allies' radar. We'll have to get the materials to Berlin via smaller cities... Ones that are not vulnerable to air strikes. It may take a little longer, but the less trafficked supply lines are the safest alternative."

Olivia nodded, taking mental notes on everything Hans said as she took a seat across the table from him. This new information didn't include the precise dates and hours she had hoped for, but it was still something. Finding out how they planned to carry all of these materials would undoubtedly be beneficial to Harold and Cecilia's bosses.

"I hope Franklin isn't giving you too much trouble at work," Hans said as he took another drink from his cup, easily shifting the topic. "I know there's been a lot more expected of you with all the extra briefings and meetings."

"Oh, Mr. Mills?" She shook her head and smiled softly. "Not too much."

"Well if he does let me know."

98

THE SECRET COURIER

"I don't need you to fight my battles you know," She cocked a sardonic brow at him, attempting to hide the grin that was growing on her lips.

"Oh, believe me, I know," he grinned, lifting his cup in a faux toast to her before sipping his drink. "Honestly I'd just like a reason to mess with Franklin Mills."

"I get the impression you don't care about him," she giggled.

"That feeling of yours would be correct," he said with a smile. "I've never much cared for people who exert their power over others for the hell of it."

"He does seem a bit power hungry, doesn't he?"

"He's a bully," Hans informed her, his tone rich with hatred that had not been there before.

"Well," Olivia smiled sweetly, grasping Hans's now-empty teacup and rising to her feet. "I'm not easily bullied." She moved passed him, squeezing his arm softly, and placed the empty cup in the kitchen sink.

A hand rested on her shoulder, sending a new wave of butterflies through her stomach as it went down the length of her arm before gripping her hand. When she turned back, she saw Hans's towering body. His contemptuous demeanor was entirely gone, and his eyes scrutinized her face in the same manner they had earlier that day at the pond.

THE SECRET COURIER

"This might be a bit preemptive, but when can I see you again?"
He asked, squeezing her hand gently.

"Well, we do work together," she said, smirking.

"Not what I mean," he said with a smile.

"Then how does dinner Friday night sound?"

"Wonderful," he grinned, his eyes gleaming like they had before he kissed her. He let go of her hand and reached up to tuck a stray strand of hair behind her ear.

She gasped, swallowing the butterflies that were rising from her stomach. His fingers lingered on her cheek, as his face moved slowly towards hers. Standing on her tiptoes, she closed the little gap between them, pushing her lips against his. He pushed the hand on her face back into her hair and interlaced his fingers inside her curls, any further efforts to glean information she may have made melting away as he returned her kiss.

14

CHAPTER FOURTEEN

Olivia went along the sidewalk, the harsh cold burning her cheeks as a gust of wind swept through the air. She adjusted her scarf and looked down the street, seeing a tall, shadowy silhouette of a guy whose face was veiled by the night sky. Her gut squeezed with a sudden sense of terror, and she had no idea why. She quickened her speed and slid around the street corner, going onto a dimly lighted alleyway. Peering over her shoulder, the dark figure was close behind, narrowing the gap between them with each step he took. She took off her shoes, gripping them in one hand, and tried to make a dash for it, only to collide with the cold, wet surface of a brick wall that had suddenly appeared out of thin air... A dead end.

The shadow resumed his approach, with the street lights overhead putting a light on his face.

Her gut constricted as her gaze landed on a familiar set of emerald eyes. The police who had assaulted her stood before her, his piercing green eyes staring at her like they had that night in the alley. Bright crimson blood coated the front of his uniform jacket, but the way he was stalking towards her now, it didn't seem that he had been injured at all, much alone shot in the abdomen.

She unclasped her backpack and brought out her weapon, aiming it at the tall soldier. She wasted no time and fired the trigger... click. She pulled it again, this time with a click. The guy was now just a few steps away, his eyes blazing with hatred and fixed only on Olivia.

"Come on!" She wailed, pushing the trigger a third time, but it was ineffective. The gun misfired again just as the soldier approached her, snatching the handgun from her fingers and throwing it to the side. Her back met the wall with a hard thud as the soldier squeezed her throat, causing her lungs to burn from a lack of air.

This was not genuine... This could not be genuine. He was

THE SECRET COURIER

dead... She had seen him breathe his last breath. She clamped her eyes tight, determined to wake up from this nightmare. How did this happen? She opened her eyes and saw her attacker's scary look. She needed to fight. She needed to get away, but her body appeared frozen by the soldier's hold. She could not raise her arms or move her legs.

Her vision faded as unconsciousness threatened to overwhelm her. She blinked furiously, attempting to dispel the haze, and the soldier's silhouette gradually returned to view as her eyesight cleared. She fixed her sight on the man's glinting green eyes, only to be greeted with a piercing blue.

Her attacker's brutish, bulky form had given way to Hans's slim, muscular physique, his fingers still firmly clutching her neck. His blue eyes pierced into hers, not with the warmth she had come to expect from his gaze, but with a savage wrath as his hold tightened around her neck. She stared, motionless, as Hans lifted his other hand, a gleam of silver flashing in the street light as cold metal pushed against her brow. Simply click... She tightened her eyes as he cocked the pistol, ready for what was to follow.

Bang! - Olivia startled awake in bed, gripping her neck, the sensation of a hand clenching around it still vivid on her skin. Her chest heaved, desperate for the breath that her nightmare

THE SECRET COURIER

had deprived her of. It was just a dream.... "It was just a dream," she said aloud, trying to calm her beating heart.

Only a dream...

***

"Are you alright?" Cecilia's words jolted Olivia out of her reverie. Olivia nodded, forcing the best grin she could make. Despite her exhaustion from lack of sleep, she managed to get out of bed in time for her appointment with Harold and Cecilia. The meeting had gone reasonably quickly. She had provided them the information she had obtained from Hans on the shipments, and that was about it.

Harold was happy, complaining less than usual, which would have lightened Olivia's day if it hadn't been for memories of the dead solider, drenched in his own blood, still playing through her mind... Or the sound of Hans's gunshots still echoed in her ears.

Harold had departed for a meeting with his superiors almost as soon as she concluded her report, eager to communicate the fresh knowledge, leaving Olivia and Cecilia to end with niceties.

"It appears that something is on your mind," Cecilia urged.

"When you first started..." Olivia trailed off, thinking hard about how to continue. "Have you had nightmares? About what you'd

THE SECRET COURIER

seen and done?

"I did," Cecilia said, her brow furrowing in slight alarm.

"Do they ever stop?" She inquired, hoping her voice would stay calm.

"I'd be lying if I said they did," she groaned. "This profession requires a lot from you, but it gets easier. Harold would describe it as compartmentalizing... I call it learning to cope," she said, smiling sympathetically. "If you want to talk about it....,"

"I'd rather try to forget about it," Olivia interrupted, shifting her sight to the window and focusing on the men and women going along the sidewalk outside.

"Our area of work is difficult, and not allowing it to drive you insane is half the fight... But we are not machines, Olivia." Cecilia spoke slowly, as if she was considering her words carefully. "You can't keep pretending there's nothing wrong... Trust me; I've tried."

"It's the soldier," Olivia said after a lengthy pause, her gaze focused on the street outside. "I can see his face everywhere... And it seems I can't even avoid him in my fantasies anymore."

"You were defending yourself," Cecilia said, reaching out and resting a soft palm on her knee. "You can't agonize over the decision to take his life when it was your own at stake."

"I know I did what needed to be done... This does not affect the realities of what I accomplished."

She shook her head, returning her focus to Cecilia and choking back the tears she thought she had already shed.

"The fact is I killed someone ... The fact is my finger pulled the trigger that stopped someone's heart."

"You can't think about it that way," Cecilia said, shaking her head. "It will eat away at you until there's nothing left if you do."

THE SECRET COURIER

15

CHAPTER FIFTEEN

"Oh no," Hans said as they neared the German restaurant he had intended to take her to. The two had met at the back entrance of the War Office as soon as the afternoon's final meeting had ended, and had strolled the few streets to Katerschmaus, a tiny German restaurant that had opened to suit the inflow of German troops now residing in Den Haag.

"Well," he said, peering through the glass into the dark, empty dining room. "Looks like they're closed for the evening," he grumbled, pulling the door handle one final time before turning to face her.

"I suppose you'll have to treat me to an old-fashioned German

THE SECRET COURIER

meal some other time," she shrugged, smiling reassuringly.

"Maybe not..." he said, furrowing his brow in consideration.

"What are you thinking?" She questioned, raising an eyebrow.

"Come with me," he said coyly. He grabbed her hand and took her along the street. They walked a few more streets together until they reached the East side of town, where they stopped at a one-story brick home.

"Where are we?"

"My house," Hans said, fidgeting with the keys in his pocket. "If I can't take you out for some good German food, we'll just make it," he said, inserting a key into the lock and twisting the knob.

"We?" she inquired, lifting her eyebrow.

"You're going to help me," he grinned, unlocking the door and motioning for her to come in.

She climbed the front stairs and strolled in the door, taking in her new surroundings. His dwelling was charming, with light blue walls. A forest green couch sat in the center of the room on a threadbare rug, with a dark wood coffee table in front of it. The space seemed desolate, with the walls stripped of any adornment save the curtains that hung over the windows. The coffee and end tables lacked the usual books and photos.

The house's individuality seems to have been taken away, leaving just the minimal requirements.

He was probably renting, she reasoned, sliding her palm over the soft fabric of the couch. Or, her chest constricted as a worse notion entered her mind: this had been a home stolen from a Jewish family forced to go to the ghettos. Her mind was filled with images of terrified individuals taking every emotional asset they possessed, leaving behind those that were too bulky or petty to go with.

"It's not much," Hans's voice said, bringing her back to reality. "But it's home."

"It's lovely," she said, attempting a grin.

"Come on," he gestured for her to follow him. "The kitchen's this way."

"So, what are we going to make?" She inquired, turning the corner into the kitchen.

"Sauerbraten," Hans said, peering over the fridge door. Shifting things about, he started bringing out different items and placing them on the countertop.

"And just what on Earth is that?" She inquired skeptically.

"You'll see," he laughed as he closed the refrigerator.

"You know, I can't really help you if you don't tell me what we're making," she said, taking up a bottle of red wine vinegar Hans had taken from a cupboard.

THE SECRET COURIER

"Well, I assume you know how to peel these?" He shot back, removing the bottle from her grip and replaced it with a carrot.

"Fine," she sighed in feigned exasperation, accepting the knife he had given to her. "Have it your way." Turning towards the counter, she began peeling and quartering the carrots. "All done," she said, scooping the carrot fragments with two hands.

"Put them in here," Hans said, pointing to the enormous cast-iron Dutch oven that had emerged on the stovetop.

As she poured the chopped carrots into the Dutch oven, she noticed the black liquid at the bottom of the pot.

"What's this?" She inquired; her nose filled with the pungent aroma of vinegar as she inhaled the mysterious mixture.

"It's the marinade for this," he said, holding up the cast iron skillet he'd been working on, the sizzling of grilled beef echoing across the kitchen. He slid the seared steak into the Dutch oven and secured the cover.

"Put that in the oven," he said, returning the pan to the burner before opening the oven.

She lifted the heavy cast iron off the burner and put it into the lowest rack, shutting the door when she was finished.

"What now?" She inquired, turning to Hans for more instructions.

THE SECRET COURIER

"Now," he continued, placing his arm around her waist and gently tugging her towards him. "We wait."

***

"That was amazing!" Olivia remarked, setting her fork down on the table. Dinner had ended about a half hour ago, and they had spent no time setting the table and eating.

"I told you," Hans laughed, setting his fork down as well.

"You could've just told me we were having the German version of pot roast, you know," she said as she sipped from her wine glass.

"This way was much more amusing, though," he grinned, rising to his feet and taking up their empty plates. He turned on his heel and vanished into the kitchen, reappearing moments later with the bottle of wine they had been enjoying.

"More?" he said, referring to her half-empty glass.

"Just a little," she smiled, putting her glass out for him to refill. He tipped over the bottle and filled hers before topping off his own.

"Come on," he urged, setting down the bottle and reaching out his hand.

Taking his hand, she rose up and followed him back into the sitting room. Sitting on the couch, she set her glass on the end table and watched Hans move over to the record player in the

111

THE SECRET COURIER

corner, one of the few personal items in the room. Flipping it on, he took up the needle and put it on the record, and soothing jazz music began to play. Turning around, he returned to where she sat and extended his hand once again.

"Come on," he said in response to her inquisitive expression.

She stood up again, this time holding his hand.

"What are you doing?" She chuckled as he placed his drink down and drew her close.

"Dancing with you," he smiled, laying his hand on her waist.

"I'm afraid I'm not much of a dancer," she giggled, tipping her head up to face him.

He shook his head, "Nonsense, have you ever tried it before?"

"Of course, I've tried it," she said, narrowing her eyes in feigned anger.

"Well, then, I'll teach you," he sneered at her. He grabbed her free hand and put it on his shoulder. Slipping his arm back around her waist, he drew her in closer, bringing their intertwined hands to chest height.

"Now," he whispered into her ear, sending shivers down her spine as his breath caressed her neck.

"Just move your feet with mine." They gradually started to swing back and forth, their feet stepping into the sink beside one

112

THE SECRET COURIER

another's. "There you go," he said, smiling down at her.

"I don't think it's that hard," she answered, mirroring his grin. She relaxed somewhat, moving her hand from his shoulder and around his neck as they began to move. Leaning forward, he laid his forehead on hers, his gaze still focused on her.

She looked down, an anxious knot in her gut tightening beneath his earnest stare. He unclasped her hand and pressed it against his chest before grabbing her chin and slowly turning her gaze back up to his. He watched her, his eyes moving over her face, taking in every detail as if she may vanish at any time. Her pulse was racing, and the air in her lungs felt as thick as cement as she struggled to regulate her breathing.

"You seem nervous," he remarked quietly, drawing little circles over the small of her back with his thumb.

"I don't think nervous is the right word," he chuckled softly. She took a long breath and shifted her gaze back to the floor.

"You make it hard for me to think straight."

"I can stop," he answered, removing his arm from around her waist.

"I don't want you to," she said, returning her attention to his. He peered down at her, his gaze seeking hers for confirmation, before putting his arm back around her waist and tugging her towards him. He leaned closer, cupping her face with his palm

THE SECRET COURIER

and almost connecting their noses.

She closed her eyes as their lips touched, his hand on the small of her back drawing her in closer, their bodies crushed together. His lips left hers, leaving a trail of kisses down the crook of her neck, her breath caught in her throat as they moved up her jaw, to her ear, and back down.

Her head became foggy as he pressed kisses across her flesh. She raised her hand from his chest and slid her other arm around his neck, weaving her fingers through the hair at his nape. His hands grasped her hips tightly as he brought his lips up to meet hers, kissing her harder and more urgently than before.

BANG! A huge explosion erupted from outside, and their mouths parted as they looked to see where the sound was coming from.

"What was that?" Olivia inquired breathlessly, her pulse still beating as the room surrounding them regained focus.

"I don't know," Hans said, advancing towards the door while keeping one arm tightly over her. They stood in quiet for a minute, listening for any additional signals of danger; the only sound in the room was the soothing melody of the record playing in the background.

"Wait here," he murmured after a few more moments of stillness.

THE SECRET COURIER

Letting go of her, he made his way to the front door, retrieving the handgun he had pulled and put on the end table when they arrived. He turned the knob and went outside, the door shutting softly behind him.

Olivia remained still, her heart beating with panic rather than the anxious anticipation of earlier. What had triggered the explosion? Were they being attacked? She took a long breath, attempting to hush the anxiety in her head. After a few more torturous minutes of stillness, Hans twisted the door knob, and it creaked open as he went inside.

"Is everything okay?" Olivia asked hastily, taking a reflexive step towards him.

"Dutch Resistance set off a bomb across town," Hans responded, returning his rifle to its original position on the table. "The building was abandoned, so no one was hurt, but they're instituting a town curfew until we catch the people behind this."

Olivia stopped off, gazing at the clock, 9:30. It was getting late, anyhow. "I suppose I should get home then."

"I'm afraid that's not going to be possible," Hans said, smiling sympathetically.

"What do you mean?" She inquired, furrowing her brow in perplexity.

THE SECRET COURIER

"The curfew is effective immediately. Everyone is to shelter in place for the night," he said, shrugging.

"What am I going to do then?"

"I suppose you'll have to stay here tonight."

16

CHAPTER SIXTEEN

Olivia gasped and sat straight up in bed. Wiping away the beads of perspiration on her forehead, she attempted to block out the pictures that had awakened her from her dream.

It was the same nightmare that had been haunting her dreams for over a month - a bloody soldier from the alley grasping her throat and pointing a gun at her temple - and she had grown accustomed to it, knowing that a variation of the same nightmare would undoubtedly occur when she closed her eyes to sleep. She turned on the light on the bedside table and gazed around Hans's bedroom, attempting to calm her beating heart.

THE SECRET COURIER

Soon after the explosion that triggered the obligatory curfew, Hans had taken her to his bedroom, suggesting she sleep on his bed while he slept on the couch. He gave her a kiss on the forehead before going to the living room for the night, dressed in a t-shirt and flannel pajama trousers.

Sighing, she flung back the blankets and got to her feet. She looked about, taking in her surroundings. Hans's bedroom was much like the rest of his home, devoid of hardly any personal belongings. Walking to the dresser, she took up the lone photo frame that was on top of it. Examining the black and white photograph, her gaze was drawn to a man and lady with three tiny children. The guy was tall, with strong shoulders and sculpted jaw. The lady was slender, with fair hair and eyes that matched Hans's. Olivia assumed the three little children were Hans's siblings. She smiled at the oldest of the children. Hans couldn't have been more than eleven or twelve when the image was shot.

Looking up from the picture, she saw a quiet, muffled voice coming from down the corridor. She returned the frame to the dresser and approached the door, gently twisting the handle as another muffled voice sounded from the living room. As she moved along the hallway, her gaze landed on Hans, who was laying on the couch, his forehead twisted in agony.

"Matthew," he said, throwing his head to one side. "No... Matthew," he said, this time louder.

"Hans," Olivia said, resting her hand on his shoulder. "Hans," she said, carefully shaking him as he continued to toss and turn. A hand suddenly gripped her arm and yanked her forward violently. Her gaze met Hans's blue eyes, which were staring up at her, his grasp on her arm tightening as the nightmare he was experiencing persisted. "Hi, Hans! It's Olivia!" She stated this, hoping he would notice her.

His eyes opened as if he had awoken from the spell that had held him prisoner, and his strong grasp on her arm was suddenly released.

"Olivia," he murmured, sitting up and looking at the crimson ring his palm had formed around her forearm.

"Are you okay?" He inquired, reaching out to touch her. "I didn't mean-,"

"I'm okay," she interrupted him off, offering him a comforting gesture. "Are you okay?"

"I am," He answered, lying back against the sofa's arm.

"Was it a nightmare?" She inquired, perched on the edge of the couch. Hans nodded.

THE SECRET COURIER

"They come so often now, I suppose you could just call it sleeping," he muttered, his shoulders dropping slightly.

"Who is Matthew?" Olivia inquired tentatively. Hans looked at her with a surprised expression on his face. "You were calling out to him in your sleep," she stated.

"Matthew was my brother's name," he said simply, his voice steady and firm.

"Oh," she replied, looking away. Hans had mentioned his brother earlier, saying that he had died while serving in the war, but that was about all he had told her. "Do you want to talk about it?"

"I'd rather just try and forget," he muttered, his gaze averted from hers.

"It helps to talk," she replied quietly, resting her hand on his arm. "Believe me ... It does."

"When I was in France, I was captain over a division just north of Calais, and my brother was stationed about twenty minutes south of me," he said after a brief pause. He swung his legs around to sit on the couch, then bowed down, putting his elbows on his knees.

"We got information that a small company of British troops was withdrawing to Dunkirk. Our instructions were to intercept and

THE SECRET COURIER

halt the business before it reached the shore. So, my guys and I linked up with my brother's division and headed north," he said.

"What we didn't know was that small company of British soldiers had already been intercepted... By a French battalion of 200 men," he said as he walked away. "We were outnumbered from the start... Surrounded on all sides, stuck in a field of landmines." He shook his head, immersed in the events of that day.

"I wish I could say I was worried about the men I had been entrusted to lead ... That everybody in a German uniform I turned over, I wasn't praying it was anyone but Matthew ... But I was," he said with a sigh.

"Then I saw him..." About twenty yards distant, pulling a wounded soldier across the field. I called out his name, and he glanced at me. Then, as quickly as his eyes focused on mine, he was gone... Blown rearward around 50 feet by a detonated ordnance." He breathed hard, the words spilling out easily now, as if they had been anxious to get away for so long.

"I knew there was nothing I, or any army doctor, could do to save him... But I raced to him nonetheless. He wasn't as wounded or bruised as you would expect from someone who had been blown up. He looked like he was sleeping... I knew he wasn't there, I knew he had left."

Olivia swallowed hard, fighting down the lump that had formed in her throat.

Hans had seen his brother die in front of his eyes, which was siOliviar to what Olivia had observed when her father and brother were slaughtered. She sympathized with Hans. She knew how it felt to lose someone you care about so unexpectedly.

"I was frozen... I couldn't think or move. If it hadn't been for the lieutenant who took me off that field, I would have perished there as well," Hans murmured, his eyes welling up with regret as he remembered the events that still tormented him.

"I had promised my mother before we went for France. I promised to bring Matthew home safely," he rang his hands together, clenching and unclenching his jaw as he summoned the fortitude to go on.

"When it was all said and done, I couldn't even bring him home," he shook his head and pressed his eyes closed. "I left him there..." I left him laying in the dirt alone."

Olivia took his hand in hers and squeezed it. "It was not your fault... There was nothing you could do," she continued, knowing full well that her words would provide little consolation.

"I understand that... It does not make it any simpler to live with, however." He shook his head and looked up at her for the first time since he began speaking. Olivia nodded slightly.

She nearly said the same thing Cecilia said when she insisted it wasn't her fault.

"I have nightmares, too," she whispered gently, catching his eyes. "That is why I heard you yell out in yours... I'd already awakened up from mine."

"What do you see in yours?" He questioned, leaning back against the couch to get a good look at her.

"Occasionally, my father and brother... Other times, the guy attacks me," she said, taking a long breath. She hoped she could tell him everything. How she'd seen her father and brother's killings... How she murdered the soldier in the alley and how it tormented her every night - but she couldn't tell him everything... She would have to bear those things alone.

"Then there are things my brain has completely made up... Something dreadful is going to happen to Grace or me," she pushed the horrific ideas aside. "If the war has given me anything, it isn't a lack of imagination for all the horrible things that can happen to a person." She looked away, a bitter chuckle leaving her lips. A hand grabbed hers, giving it a gentle squeeze. She gazed up at Hans, who studied her with understanding

THE SECRET COURIER

rather than pity.

"At the risk of sounding as though my intentions aren't pure, would you like to sleep in here tonight?"

He inquired sincerely, albeit his lips curled into a faint grin. "I'll sleep on the floor, of course," he said, his grin growing.

"Well," she grinned, and the weight in her chest lifted somewhat. "I suppose there's no harm in it if you'll be on the floor."

He sat down on the floor and patted the couch. Her grin broadened as she lay down, drawing the blanket over herself. She observed Hans take a throw pillow from the chair and another blanket before resting down on the floor next to the couch.

"Goodnight, Hans," she said, reaching down and grabbing his hand, her eyelids flickering as tiredness overcame her.

"Goodnight, Olivia," he said, holding her hand.

17

CHAPTER SEVENTEEN

"You mean to tell me, you spent the night with this man, and you still couldn't manage to get any other information from him?" Harold yelled across the Winslows' sitting room.

Olivia awakened on Hans's couch soon as the morning light started to shine through the windows. She had sneaked out the front door unobserved after changing back into her outfit from the night before, stepping over Hans's sleeping figure, stepping the quarter mile back to her house, she bathed and dressed before gulping down a pretty large cup of coffee and stepping out the door again.

THE SECRET COURIER

She had been sitting in the Winslow's sitting room ever after Harold's evident dissatisfaction at the paucity of information she had gained from her night with 'the captain.'

"I told you," she started with tight teeth. "Staying the night wasn't the plan..."

"I don't care if it was the bloody plan!" Harold shouted. "Use it to your advantage!"

"Harold..." Cecilia interjected, apparently uncomfortable with what Harold had just suggested.

"No Cat," he interrupted her. "She wanted this job... She came to us, not the other way around," he said, turning back to face Olivia. "Do you think other agents get treated the way you do?" He inquired, raising a condescending eyebrow.

"Do you think their handlers coach them on every move they make before they make it?"

"Harold..." Cecilia started again.

"Because they don't - They're on their own!" He proceeded. "You requested for this position... You asked to be a SIS agent; it's about time you started acting like one!"

"Harold!" Cecilia said again, more fiercely this time.

"No, Cecilia," Olivia said. "He's right." Harold and Cecilia returned her gaze, each with a bewildered expression. "Any other agent would've had the information you need by now," she went on to say.

"I've been playing it too safe with Captain Friedrich."

That was true... She had played it cautious with Hans. In part because she was afraid of being discovered. However, if she were honest with herself, it wasn't the only reason. Despite her better judgment, she had actually enjoyed her time with Hans. When she was with him, she could easily lose track of herself... It was easy to forget the conflict that had enveloped the world around them for the previous three years.

"I asked you something before we ever started this arrangement," Harold said, his tone somewhat less aggressive than before. "I asked if you could separate yourself from your emotions - if you could detach yourself from any feelings that might develop," he said, sitting in the recliner opposite from Olivia. He leaned forward and put his elbows on the tops of his knees, staring at her closely.

"I'll ask you again, and please be honest with me. Can you do this job?"

"I can," Olivia said, answering Harold's passionate look.

"Then start acting like it, and get me information on those transports," he said, taking a long draw from the tumbler of scotch on the end table beside him.

THE SECRET COURIER

"Don't be reckless, but do what has to be done."

18

CHAPTER EIGHTEEN

"Where were you the other morning? I woke up and you had vanished," Hans's voice said from behind Olivia, causing her to jump and almost drop the cup of coffee she had just poured herself.

"I was worried about you," he said.

"I didn't think it would be wise to be seen leaving your house so early in the morning, so I slipped out before anyone could notice," she said with a grin. She knew Hans would ask her where she had run off to at some point, but the hectic morning of meetings they had sat through had prevented them from conversing.

THE SECRET COURIER

"You should've woken me up," he insisted.

"You had such a long night, and I didn't want to bother you," she lied again.

"Well, I still wish you would've let me walk you home," he said, but it seemed that her response had been sufficient for him not to push any further. "Especially with the people who set off the bomb still out there."

"They still haven't been caught?" Olivia inquired with false curiosity, attempting to shift the topic.

"They have been now," he said. "I was called into work shortly after you departed. We captured them yesterday night... A few of youngsters were no older than seventeen. I will never comprehend it... Destroying your own city to prove a point," Hans said, shaking his head.

"Humph," she nodded, attempting a pleasant grin. Deg Haag was not the Dutch people's city... Not anymore. It was lost, along with the rest of the nation, when the Germans invaded Holland. "What will happen to them?"

"Well, no one was hurt so I imagine they'll be sent to a labor camp," Hans said with a smirk. Olivia averted her gaze, her thoughts turning to Grace; the children responsible for the explosion were no older than she was. "Are you alright?" Hans

THE SECRET COURIER

inquired, resting a hand on her shoulder. "You seem preoccupied."

"I'm fine," she shook her head, seeming to grin. "Just a lot left to do before I go home for the day," she lied, but it wasn't completely false. She had completed drafting out the minutes from that morning's meeting, as well as the schedule for tomorrow, hours ago, and had been spending all of her efforts on figuring out how to acquire Hans's transportation details.

"Well, I won't keep you from your work for much longer," Hans said, his worried look turning into a grin. "About the other night," he started in a quiet voice, looking around to make sure they were alone. "I never got the chance to thank you."

"You don't have to thank me," she said, shaking her head and waving her hand at him.

"I've never discussed my brother in that manner with anybody. You were correct... It helped," he continued, nodding in gratitude.

"And," he said, grasping her hand softly in his. "If you ever need to talk, I'd love to listen."

"Thank you," she said, smiling at him. "Ahem," she cleared her throat when he didn't release her hand after a few moments.

"Right... Well," he released her hands and looked around to make sure they were still alone. "I do not want to be late for my

THE SECRET COURIER

meeting. I'll see you later, Ms. Carter." He grinned.

"Captain Friedrich," she nodded, matching his smile.

Hans turned and went out of the break room, vanishing behind a pair of double doors at the end of the corridor. Olivia returned to her workstation by turning on her heel and walking in the other direction. Opening the blue folder she had left on her desk before her break, she started perusing the agenda she had drawn out for tomorrow's meeting, her thoughts returning to her intentions to collect the transportation locations. Hans had openly shared the information she had previously provided the Winslows. She had gotten it out of him with some casual chat... However, something told her that the details, such as times and places, would not be as simply discussed over dinner.

"I just need to drop off these files on Operation Workhorse, and then I'll be ready to go," Olivia heard from across the room. Looking up from her documents, she saw Lieutenants Cooper and Spencer. She knew them both from General Sinclair's regular briefings, but she had never talked to either of them personally. She was aware, however, that Lieutenant Cooper had been attending the special meetings on the supply deliveries to Berlin. She looked at the dossier he was holding at his side: Operation Workhorse... She couldn't recollect having heard that

THE SECRET COURIER

name before. Could this be the codename for the Stalingrad rescue effort?

She observed from the corner of her eye as Lieutenant Cooper strolled across the room to the General's office. Turning the door, he strolled inside, returning a second later with the folder no longer in his grasp.

She kept an eye on Cooper as he moved back across the room to Spencer, and the two walked out of the building together. Looking up from her desk, she looked around the room. Except for her, the office was entirely empty; the rest of the typists had already left for the evening, and Olivia had never been asked to the afternoon conference with the remaining officers.

Looking around for anybody else, she rose up from her seat and grabbed the folder she was pretending to glance over. She needed to know what was in the file Lieutenant Cooper was holding. It may very possibly contain the answers she urgently sought... And if she could acquire them without implicating Hans, that would be ideal. Gliding across the room, she reached General Sinclair's door, glanced back one final time before twisting the knob and slipping inside.

She hurriedly approached his desk, her pulse pounding like a drum against her ears. Her eyes combed the piles of papers and

THE SECRET COURIER

folders atop the dark chestnut till she saw it: a bright red folder with the words Operation Workhorse printed across the front.

Looking towards the door, she opened the file and swiftly scanned the first page.

"January 11th... Arnhem... January 13th... Bocholt... January 15th... Essen," she read, bits of dates and locales appearing as she scanned the pages. She felt certain that she had found the information she was searching for. Flipping through a few more pages, she examined the numerous maps that had been drawn up, indicating the route the transport trucks would travel.

"Thank you, Captain," she heard General Sinclair say from outside the door. She closed the folder and grabbed the file she had brought in with her just before General Sinclair opened the office door.

"Ms. Carter," he began, astonishment on his face as his gaze fell on her.

"Oh, hello, sir," she replied with the best grin she could manage.

"I - um - finished the agenda for tomorrow a little early," she said, bringing out the blue folder.

"I didn't want to disrupt your meeting, so I thought I'd sneak it into your office before I went for the evening... I hope that's okay," she said, looking up at him innocently.

134

"Of course," he said, his expression settling into a comfortable grin.

"Well," she murmured, edging past him as she headed for the door. "I suppose I should get going."

"Ms. Carter," General Sinclair said from behind her.

With her pulse beating, she turned to face him. "Yes sir?"

"The agenda?" he said, referring to the file she was still holding in her hand.

"Oh, of course," she chuckled uneasily. "I'm sorry... It's been a hard day," she said, handing him the folder with an apologetic grin.

"Not a problem," he said, shaking his head. "I hope you'll get plenty of rest for tomorrow. We have another long day of meetings."

"Of course, sir," she said, the nausea in her stomach subsiding somewhat.

"Thank you." With that, she exited the office, her legs feeling as if they were about to give way at any minute. That was too close. Reaching her desk, she started collecting her belongings, not wanting to spend any more time before leaving.

"In trouble with the boss?" A familiar voice said from behind her.

She turned around and looked at Lieutenant Hayesn.

"No... Why would you say that?" She inquired, her tone

becoming more defensive than she had meant.

"Relax," he laughed, leaning against her desk. "I was only joking."

"I was just giving General Sinclair the agenda for tomorrow morning's briefing before I leave for the day," she said, returning her focus to packing her belonging.

"Well, I'm glad I caught you then," he replied, a sneer visible in his voice.

"There are some high-ranking officials coming to visit next week and there's going to be a banquet held in their honor."

The knot in Olivia's gut tightened... She understood where this was headed.

"Considering you still haven't let me take you out, I was wondering-," He continued, but she stopped him short.

"Oh, Lieutenant Hayesn," she started, turning to face him with the sorriest grin she could summon. "I'm not sure that's such a good idea..."

"There'll be dancing... champagne," he said, dismissing her concerns.

"I'm afraid I'm already going with someone," she confessed.

"Oh," he murmured, his grin turning into a scowl. "Who?"

"A... Friend," she lied, biting her cheek as a flush spread over her

THE SECRET COURIER

chest and neck.

"A friend?" He inquired; his brow arched with skepticism.

"Yes," she nodded firmly.

"Well... Save a dance for me then," he replied, his smile returning as he lifted himself from her desk, his gaze running over her body one final time before vanishing out the door.

19

CHAPTER NINETEEN

Olivia sat across from Hans, watching him go through a stack of paperwork on his desk. They'd been stuck in his office all evening because Hans had mounds of paperwork to catch up on before the end of the week. Because it would be her last opportunity to see him over the weekend, she had accepted his request to stay late with him while he worked. She took a drink from her whiskey glass and watched him study each piece of paper, making comments in the margins here and there.

"Are you going to the banquet next Friday?" She inquired after they had sat in quiet for a time. She had been intending to

THE SECRET COURIER

question him about the dinner ever since Lieutenant Hayesn had asked her, but the week had been too hectic for her to have another minute alone with him.

"How do you know about that?" He gazed up at her with a puzzled expression.

"I was asked to go," she said nonchalantly.

"Oh really?" He inquired, "Well, that's a shame because I had planned to ask you myself," he shrugged, a slight grin forming on the edges of his lips.

"Well, that's a relief, given that I told him I was already going with someone else," she said, a smile appearing on her lips.

"So, you just assumed I was going to ask you?" He inquired, raising an eyebrow at her.

"Well, at this point, it would certainly be inconvenient if I had to find someone else to take me," she shrugged, her smile deepening.

"Did Lieutenant Hayes ask you?" He inquired simply, with amusement on his face.

"How'd you know?" She inquired, giving him a probing look this time.

"Just a guess," Hans said, smirking. "He seems to fancy you quite a bit."

"I hadn't noticed," Olivia said cynically.

139

THE SECRET COURIER

Hans laughed, scrolling over his notes and taking a sip on his cigarette.

"That's a horrible habit, you know," she said.

"Have you ever tried one?" He questioned, raising an eyebrow.

She shook her head, staring at the brilliant orange flames that lighted up as Hans inhaled another puff of smoke and gently blew it out the side of his lips.

"Here," he said, removing the ash that had begun to build on the end of the cigarette before handing it to her.

"I... don't know," she murmured, staring between him and the cigarette with concern.

"I don't think I'd be much good at it."

He shook his head, "Nonsense, just hold it between these two fingers," he said, raising his index and middle fingers.

"And breath in like you're drinking out of a straw."

She stopped for a while, narrowing her eyes in thought, before accepting the cigarette from him. She brought it up to her lips and took a big suck, the smoke stinging her throat and lungs as she inhaled. She coughed heavily and held it out for Hans to grab.

"That was awful," she continued, clearing her throat and brushing away the tears that had started to gather in her eyes.

THE SECRET COURIER

"I suppose it's not for everyone," he joked, reclaiming the cigarette from her.

"I think I'll stick to this as my guilty pleasure," she added, holding up the glass of scotch whiskey she had been sipping throughout the evening.

"It looks like you could use some more," he added, pointing to her half empty glass.

"That's all right," she said, waving her hand at him.

"I insist," he said, taking the bottle from his desk and uncorking it. "I'd need a second glass too if I had been sitting here all night watching someone do paperwork."

"Well, I suppose one more won't hurt anything," she said, holding out her glass for him to pour her another hearty portion of Scotch before pouring himself one as well.

"It's been fun," she remarked, sipping from her glass.

"You don't have to lie," he joked, shutting the file he had been reading and putting it in the top drawer on his desk.

"All finished?"

"Not even close," Hans said, pushing back his chair and rising to his feet. He extinguished his cigarette in the ashtray, collected his glass, and around the desk, offering his empty hand to her.

"But I think it's time for a break."

"Where are we going?" She asked, taking his hand and allowed him to lift her up from her chair.

"You'll see," he grinned, bringing her out of his office. The War Office was abandoned, with the dazzling lights of the day replaced by the warm, fluorescent glow of the emergency lights that turned on at night after everyone had gone home. It seemed weirdly eerie being there at night, she thought as they went hand in hand down the hall, past the break room and briefing room, and down a hallway to a portion of the building Olivia had never seen before.

She followed closely as he led her up a dimly lighted staircase. Olivia looked around as she reached the top.

A large space lay before her, separated into smaller rooms by towering archways supported by ivory columns. The walls were covered with oil paintings, some of which depicted individuals, others landscapes or structures.

"What is this place?" She questioned, taking a step closer, her gaze drawn to the first artwork, a portrait of a young lady. Olivia inspected the canvas. The lady was fair-skinned, with long black hair. She donned a white tunic with a blue ribbon, and a lion sat at her side. The picture depicted The Dutch Maiden, the icon of the Dutch Rebellion.

"I discovered it on one of my late nights at the workplace." Hans

THE SECRET COURIER

stated that each artwork tells a tale about Dutch history, beginning with Independence and continuing to the present. He pointed to the depiction of The Dutch Maiden.

"Sometimes I come up here when I need to think, or need a break from work."

"It's lovely," Olivia said, letting go of Hans's hand and moving ahead, her gaze wandering over each piece as she traveled around the room.

"I can't believe these haven't been taken down," she said, looking at a painting of a ship, its brown hull standing out against the deep blue ocean that smashed around it.

"To be honest, I don't think anyone who cares enough to take them all down realizes they're up here," Hans said, studying her as she inspected each artwork.

"I'm glad," she responded, spinning around to face him.

"So am I," he said, taking a drink from his glass and placing it on the foyer table before approaching her.

They stood next to each other, scrutinizing the painting of a fair-skinned lady with red lips, a blue head scarf, and a single pearl earring on her ear. The portrait was undoubtedly a replica of the renowned Vermeer painting, yet it was nonetheless remarkable.

"It's beautiful," Hans replied, putting her hand in his.

THE SECRET COURIER

"Thank you for showing me this," she said, glancing up from the painting to see Hans's gaze on her. Her stomach knotted as a rush of fear swept over her, realizing how alone she was for the first time that night.

"Of course," he grinned, his gaze sweeping over every detail of her face.

"You look beautiful tonight... If I haven't told you yet," he whispered, coming in closer, the scent of whiskey on his breath making her pulse accelerate.

"I don't think you've mentioned it," she said anxiously, swallowing the butterflies growing in her chest.

"Well, you do," he murmured, coming in closer until their noses almost touched. She closed her eyes and mashed her lips against his. He grabbed her waist and pulled her into him as he reciprocated her kiss. She wrapped her arms around his neck and crushed her body against his, her head blurred by the usual haze that came with his touch. He raised his hand and clasped her face. He was kissing her harder and more frantically now, one hand tightly clutching her waist and the other entwined in her hair. Walking backwards, he forced her back against one of the columns, his lips leaving hers and trailing kisses down the

THE SECRET COURIER

hollow of her neck. She breathed deeply, attempting to calm her breath.

"It-it's getting late," she mumbled, attempting to clear her head of the fog that threatened to overwhelm her. Hans drew away, planting one last kiss across her collarbone and meeting her eyes. His lips parted slightly, and his eyes were filled with something she couldn't quite identify - was it longing?... Desire?

Whatever it was, it made her want to remain, a new pair of butterflies fluttering in her stomach.

"I'll walk you home," he whispered, releasing her waist and seizing her hand instead, planting a kiss on her forehead.

20

CHAPTERTWENTY

Olivia climbed the front steps of the War Office and pushed through the double doors, the faint twang of jazz entering her ears right away. Turning away from where she usually reported to work, she headed down the corridor towards the enormous banquet hall on the west wing. Smoothing down the velvet material of her emerald green dress, she breathed hard, regretting her choice to wear such a formfitting outfit. Why was she so nervous? Adjusting one of the pins that kept her hair back from her face, she tucked a curl behind her ear before turning the corner and entering into the banquet hall's arched archway.

Dozens of people packed the space, some gliding around the dance floor while others gathered to converse and drink champagne. Olivia scanned the throng for Hans. They had agreed to meet at the party since she needed to go home to prepare, and Hans needed to complete some paperwork. She wished they'd come together now. She hated feeling so out of place.

"So, where's this friend of yours?" A voice yelled behind her, sending a knot of fear into Olivia's gut.

"He's here somewhere, I'm sure," she said nonchalantly, her gaze fixed on the throng rather than Lieutenant Hayes, who was now standing at her side.

"Well while you wait for him, how about that dance?" He started by walking in front of her, blocking her view of the room.

"Oh, I'm not much of a dancer," she said, trying a grin.

"I'll teach you," he urged, grasping her hand before she could protest. "Oh, come on, it's just one dance," he continued, seeing her apprehensive demeanor. She decided it wasn't worth fighting and let Lieutenant Hayes draw her to the dance floor.

"You look beautiful tonight," he said, his gaze wandering down her form. "That dress..."

THE SECRET COURIER

"Thank you," she stopped him off with a forced grin.

"You still haven't answered my question, you know," he said calmly, pressing his hands on her waist as they swayed to the music.

"Question?" She wrinkled her brow and placed her hands stiffly on his shoulders.

"When you're going to let me take you out to dinner," he said with a sneer.

"Oh," she muttered, hoping for a response that would get him off her back without revealing too much about her and Hans's connection.

"I'm afraid I'm ... Seeing someone."

"Is he in the military?" Lieutenant Hayesn inquired, looking unperturbed by the news.

"Yes," she nodded.

"Well," he started, the same confident smile that he usually wore raising the edges of his lips. "It can't be that serious."

"Excuse me?" She inquired, surprised by his answer.

"No man in his right mind would leave a beautiful woman like you behind to go fight in a war... At least not without putting a ring on your finger," He grinned, taking her left hand in his and holding it up as if to study it. She slipped her hand out of his

THE SECRET COURIER

hold and glanced up at him, an amazed expression on her face at his sheer boldness.

"So, I'm sure one date couldn't hur-,"

"Hello, Ms. Carter," a familiar voice said, interrupting Lieutenant Hayes. Olivia turned her head, her gaze resting on Hans, who was clothed in full costume and wearing a lovely grin.

"Lieutenant Hayes," he said, nodding in his general direction but without acknowledging him further.

"I was wondering if I could trouble you for a dance?" He inquired, extending out his hand.

"I'm afraid we're not finished dancing," Lieutenant Hayes said, his grasp on her waist tightening slightly.

"With all respect, Lieutenant," Hans remarked, his cheerful manner never wavering for a moment.

"I was asking the lady."

"Well," Olivia said, looking between the two guys. "I suppose one dance couldn't hurt." Grabbing Hans's extending hand, she slid free of Lieutenant Hayes's clutches, leaving him standing alone with a frown on his face.

"You looked like you could use rescuing," Hans mumbled into her ear once they had moved far enough away.

"Did I?" She inquired, a tiny grin appearing on her lips as Hans guided her farther into the dance floor.

"Just a little," he said, casually laying his hand on her waist as they started to dance.

"Thank you," she responded sincerely. "He's quite persistent."

"He certainly is," Hans mused. "I might be a bit jealous if I didn't know you were completely uninterested."

"Just a bit?" She cocked an eyebrow.

"I'll admit," Hans said, his grin becoming wider. "I didn't love the sight of you dancing with another man ... Especially a man who seems to fancy you so much."

"You think he fancies me?" She asked cynically.

"You're practically all he talks about," he said. "He seems to be under the impression the two of you are going to have dinner soon."

"Well, I'm afraid I dashed those hopes just a moment ago," she said with a smirk.

"Told him no?" He inquired, lifting an eyebrow in faux astonishment.

"More or less," Olivia shrugged. "I told him I was seeing someone," she said, her heart skipping a beat as the words came out.

"Really?" Hans inquired calmly, the corner of his mouth twitching slightly as a grin tried to form.

THE SECRET COURIER

"Mhm," she said, her cheeks warming slightly.

"Good," he muttered, his lips curled into a little grin as his gaze swept over her face.

"You look lovely tonight, by the way," he said, bringing her closer as they swayed to the music.

"Thank you," she said, the crimson flush that had developed on her cheeks starting to spread down her neck.

"Would you like a drink?" He inquired as the sound of mellow jazz faded and the band started to play a new tune.

"Lead the way," she grinned, following Hans as he led them off the dancefloor.

"Captain Friedrich," an unknown voice said in German as they approached a table adorned with champagne flutes. They turned around and saw a muscular guy with graying hair that was thinning in the center.

"General Morrison," Hans responded, standing to attention right away.

"At ease," the guy said, a big smile spreading over his face. "How have you been my boy?" He inquired, taking Hans's hand in his own for a firm grip.

"I've been doing well," Hans said, returning the general's handshake.

THE SECRET COURIER

"I trust Den Haag is treating you well?" General Morrison inquired, still speaking in his own language. "Though I heard you had some trouble getting here," he said, his brow furrowing slightly.

"Yes, sir," Hans nodded and responded in German as well. "I managed to make it here in one piece, give or take a few new scars," he said.

General Morrison chuckled, firmly clapping Hans on the shoulder. "Well, they're lucky to have you here at the War Office."

"Thank you, sir," Hans said, smiling.

"Who do we have here?" General Morrison inquired, moving his gaze to Olivia, his pleasant grin spreading. She reddened slightly and fiddled with the straps of her dress, which hung freely from her shoulders.

"This is Olivia Carter," Hans said.

"She's quite easy on the eyes," General Morrison said, raising an eyebrow at Hans.

"It's a pleasure to meet you, General," Olivia said in German, offering her hand to General Morrison. Both men's eyes opened in astonishment when they realized she understood them, while Hans's lips twitched slightly.

"You speak German?" General Morrison questioned amusedly, taking her hand and bringing it up to his lips, placing a brief kiss before releasing it.

She nodded.

"I'm afraid I'm a bit rusty though."

"Well, it's a pleasure to meet you," General Morrison said in English, his German accent heavy.

"Likewise," Olivia said with a grin.

"Olivia is General Sinclair's personal typist," Hans said. "She attends all of the briefings at the office."

"I'm sure she keeps you on your toes," General Morrison said.

"She certainly does," Hans laughed.

"Well, I won't take up any more of your time," General Morrison said, grabbing a champagne flute from the table near them. "You two enjoy your evening."

"You, too, sir," Hans said, shaking his hand one last time.

"I didn't know you spoke German," Hans replied after they'd retrieved their drinks from the table and moved to a more private section of the banquet hall.

"I learned it as a girl," Olivia shrugged. "I know enough to carry on casual conversation... And to know when I'm being talked about," she added with a mischievous grin.

"General Morrison seemed impressed with you," Hans said, sipping from his drink. "And that's quite an accomplishment. He isn't easily impressed."

"How do the two of you know each other?" She inquired, blushing at Hans's comment as she drank from her own glass.

"He was my training officer and superior in Calais," he said, adjusting his eyes uneasily at the mention of his time in France.

"Well, he seems to think very highly of you," Olivia smiled, attempting to move the subject away from its current direction. "And if what you say is true, that's quite a feat," she said, echoing the sentence he had just spoken.

"He's actually the person who got me this job," he replied, raising his glass to his lips again. "When I put in for a transfer, he made a few calls."

She nodded, wondering what to say. Why had Hans applied for a transfer? Is it because of what happened to his brother? She wanted to inquire, but she realized it was not the time to bring up such a sensitive matter.

"I know the night's still early, but would you want to get out of here?" Hans inquired, jolting her out of her musings. "These parties aren't exactly my cup of tea," he said, smiling slightly.

THE SECRET COURIER

"Mine either," she joked, returning her grin. "But won't they realize you've left?"

"I don't think anyone will miss me," Hans grinned, referring to the throngs of people filling the dinner hall.

"Then lead the way," she smiled, setting down her drink and grasping Hans's hand.

21

CHAPTER TWENTY-ONE

"Would you like a drink?" Hans inquired, removing his uniform coat as they entered through the front entrance of his home. He went into the kitchen after laying it on the couch. They had left the celebration by sneaking out one of the dining hall's rear doors without being seen, and had strolled the few streets from the War Office to Hans's apartment.

"I'll take a whiskey," Olivia said, looking at the Knight's Cross pinned to the front of his tunic. She picked up the jacket from the couch and inspected it, recalling the first time she saw the award. "I haven't seen you wear this since the night we met," she

THE SECRET COURIER

remarked, turning the corner into the kitchen while holding Hans's jacket.

"Hmm?" Hans questioned, turning around with a tumbler of whiskey in each hand. "Oh," he murmured, his gaze settling on the Knight's Cross.

"I only wear it on special occasions. Ceremonies, banquets, and other such events."

"Why?" Olivia inquired, really curious as to why he wouldn't wear it all the time. She was certain that any other German commander would.

"Because I don't deserve it," he said simply, his tone tenser than usual.

"What do you mean you don't deserve it?" Olivia inquired; her eyebrows pulled together in perplexity. Was he pretending humility? ... Trying not to brag?

"I don't," he said bluntly, passing her glass across the table to her.

"I'm sure that's not true," she started.

"Just drop it, Olivia," he said forcefully, snatching her jacket and flinging it through the doorway back into the living room.

"Hans..." She trailed off, laying a gentle palm on his arm.

"I'm sorry," he said, running an angry palm over his face. "I didn't mean to-,"

"It's okay," she interrupted, tenderly squeezing his arm.

157

THE SECRET COURIER

"Come on," he urged, taking her hand and guiding her back into the living room. He sat down on the couch and took a big drink from his whiskey. "Do you want to know how I got that Knight's Cross?" He inquired, placing his glass on the side table.

"You don't have to-," she started.

"I want to," he told her. "The ambush my unit encountered in France ... When Matthew..." He drifted off. She nodded, indicating that he did not need to explain more. "We only suffered two casualties during the whole fight," he went on to say.

"Every other guy made it off the field, either by walking away or being carried off by a fellow soldier. Everyone dubbed me a hero... They said that it was only due of my leadership during such a crisis that no more guys were slain." He sneered, shaking his head.

"The only person who knew the truth was my Lieutenant, who had to pull me off the field," he said, taking another drink from his glass. "He understood the truth but didn't say anything... Just let everyone think it was me who took command during the attack."

"It was your brother... No one would blame you for not thinking

THE SECRET COURIER

clearly after witnessing what you did," she added, resting a hand on his knee.

"It wouldn't' have mattered," he said, shaking his head. "It was my responsibility to guide those soldiers, and I failed... The worst thing is that I was compensated for it... Honored for courage that I did not possess..." He drifted off, and stillness filled the room.

"I'm sorry," Olivia said, and she meant it. Sorry for judging him so severely the first time she discovered the Knight's Cross... Sorry for being so dishonest with him after he had been so honest with her. She hoped she could tell him everything. Who she really was... The atrocities she had done that plagued her nightmares... What she had seen.

"What's done is done," Hans replied matter-of-factly, his face less tense than before. "That's why I applied for a transfer. I could not remain in France... Not after failing so terribly and losing Matthew."

"For what it's worth," she said, scooting closer to him on the couch. "I think moving on after losing someone you love takes more bravery than any battle you could ever fight... I would know," she said gently, smiling sympathetically.

Hans grinned back at her, leaning in until their foreheads touched.

THE SECRET COURIER

"Thank you," he said quietly, laying a quick kiss on her lips.

She closed her eyes and kissed him back, her stomach in knots as she melted against his lips.

"It's getting late," he remarked, pushing away and rising to his feet, holding Olivia's hand to assist her up. "I'll walk you home."

"Or I could stay," she blurted out. Hans turned around, his eyes meeting hers.

"I'm sorry," she said, a flush crawling up her neck as she looked back at him. "That was horribly inappropriate of m-,"

"Don't be sorry," he cut in, eyeing her carefully, his eyes filled with something Olivia couldn't identify.

Slowly, he raised a hand and rested it on her face, his gaze seeking hers. He leaned forward and mashed his lips on hers.

She closed her eyes and kissed him back, her breath caught in her throat as Hans's arms slid around her waist, pressing her into him. She wrapped her arms around his neck and ran her fingers through the hair at the back of his neck. After a little pause, he pulled away and glanced down at her, his gaze returning to hers.

"You don't have to stay if you don't want to," he whispered, tucking a stray curl behind her ear and resting his hands on her

160

THE SECRET COURIER

skin.

"I want to," she responded forcefully, her voice barely audible as she attempted to control the pounding beating inside her chest. She nodded, responding to the unspoken query.

He took her hand in his, led her down the corridor, and opened the door to his bedroom. He led her inside, turned to face her, and wrapped his arms around her waist.

"Are you sure?" He questioned, looking down at her. She nodded and placed her hands on his chest. He leaned down and kissed her again, harder and more passionately. She kissed him back, rubbing her body against his as he drew her closer. His hands grasped her waist tightly, and his lips left hers, leaving a path of kisses down the hollow of her neck. She took a deep breath, her head becoming foggy as his lips stroked over her collarbone. She brought her hands up to the back of his head and hooked her fingers in his hair, leaning back as his lips touched her ear.

Her head became foggy as their lips rejoined. She let go of his hair and moved her hands back down to his chest. With shaking fingers, she started playing with his shirt buttons, her thoughts racing as his tongue touched hers. She unbuttoned his shirt one at a time, peeling it back after each one. Hans freed her waist,

THE SECRET COURIER

slipping his arms out of the sleeves, and the garment fell on the floor. Breaking their kiss, he moved back, sliding his undershirt over his head and dropped it on the floor.

Olivia glanced at him, her cheeks blushing a faint pink as she took in the sculpted muscles of his chest, her gaze drawn to the one scar just under his ribs. She had seen him without a shirt before, but not like this.

Swallowing the butterflies in her stomach, she put her hands on his chest and ran them down the length of his body, pausing when she reached the waistline of his pants.

He lifted her face to meet his gaze, placing a palm under her chin.

"Your hands are shaking," he whispered quietly, bringing hers into his own.

"Just nervous," she whispered trembling, her pulse racing.

"We can stop," he started.

"No," she said, shaking her head. "I don't want to stop."

Hans nodded, brushing his fingers on her cheeks and gently pressing his lips to hers. She kissed him back. She struggled with the belt buckle after lowering her hands to his pants. His hands held hers tenderly.

"Slow down," he murmured into her ear, his breath sending

shivers down her spine.

"You're so beautiful," Hans whispered, his gaze sweeping down her body as she turned around to face him, the chemise she had been wearing under her dress just touching her legs.

Wrapping his arms around her waist, he drew her close and moved her backwards toward the bed.

He took a step back, gently laying her down, removing his belt and unfastening his pants before slipping them down and stepping out.

"I think I love you," Hans whispered, pressing his lips against hers and meeting her eyes.

"I think I love you too," Olivia said, pushing her lips against his as the world around her faded away.

22

CHAPTER TWENTY-TWO

Olivia snapped her eyes awake as the morning light shone brightly through Hans's bedroom window.

"Good morning," Hans said against her ear, his arm wrapping around her waist and bringing her back into his chest.

"Good morning," she smiled, tipping her head around to face him.

"I trust you slept well?" He asked, kissing her temples.

"Mhm," she said, stretching her arm over her head as she lay over to face him.

"What time is it?" She inquired casually, brushing her forehead against his.

"Nearly ten," he said, moving a hair off her face and resting his palm on her cheek.

"Ten o'clock?" She repeated, lifting her eyebrows. She couldn't recall the last time she had received a full night's sleep without the interruption of her typical nightmares... She hadn't woken up once throughout the night.

"Mhm," he nodded, drawing her closer to him. "We missed breakfast, but I'm sure I could whip something up if you're hungry," he said with a smile.

"I'd love that," she grinned, kissing his lips.

Hans moved onto his back, leaning into her kiss, and pulled her onto him. She kissed him back, pressing her hands on his naked chest, her pulse pounding. Sitting up with her on his lap, he threw his arms around her, firmly holding her to him as his kisses traveled down her neck.

"J-Hans," she muttered, battling back the fog that was forming in her consciousness. Even though she wanted to remain in bed with him all day, she had a weekly Saturday appointment with the Winslows in just a few hours.

"Breakfast, remember?" She grinned as he cocked his head up to look at her.

"Right," he laughed, dropping another kiss behind her ear

before letting her slip off his lap and back to her side of the bed.

Sitting on the side of the bed, he retrieved his boxers off the floor and slipped them on before rising to his feet. Olivia's cheeks flushed slightly as she pulled the covers up to her neck, realizing she, too, was naked.

"So, what do you plan on whipping up?" She inquired, following Hans as they proceeded down the corridor.

"What would you like?" He inquired as they turned the corner into the kitchen.

"Well, coffee, for starters," she said, taking a seat at the kitchen table.

"That can be arranged," he joked, unlocking the cabinet and retrieving the coffee container. He set the kettle on the burner after filling it with grounds and water.

"As for food..." she trailed off, getting to her feet and heading to the refrigerator. Opening the door, she looked inside.

"I'm in charge of breakfast," Hans murmured to her ear, wrapping an arm around her waist and dragging her away from the refrigerator. "All you have to do is sit right here," he said, directing her back to the kitchen table. "And tell me what you want."

"Pancakes," she said, after a minute of contemplation. She accepted the cup of coffee he had prepared for her and then watched him pour one for himself.

23

CHAPTER TWENTY-THREE

Olivia went along the sidewalk, drifts of snow shoveled earlier that morning piled knee high on each side of the pavement. She wrapped her scarf over her neck, a shiver running through her as a burst of wind blew her hair back. She looked severely overdressed for a Saturday morning, wearing the same green velvet dress that had hugged her contours the night before. She hadn't had time to go home before her appointment with the Winslows, so she just buttoned her coat all the way up, the red wool covering the party dress beneath.

Climbing the familiar stairs to the Winslows' house, she

THE SECRET COURIER

knocked on the door.

The knob twisted, and the door clicked open, showing a smiling Cecilia.

"Hello," she murmured, moving aside to enable Olivia to enter.

"Hello," Olivia said, matching Cecilia's pleasant grin. Slipping her scarf off her neck, her gaze was drawn to a thin fir tree in the distant corner of the room, its branches adorned with tinsel and dazzling decorations. She almost forgot that Christmas was just a week away.

A sorrow ran through her chest as memories of her father and sibling filled her consciousness. This would be her first Christmas without them. She wondered about Grace and what she was up to at the time. Did she decorate the tree with their great aunt and cousins? Was she thinking about their father and brother? What about Olivia? She fought back tears as she realized how lonely she was. Pushing the memories aside, she cleared her throat, resuming the charming grin she had previously wore.

"The tree looks lovely," she observed, putting her scarf on the hook near the entrance and unbuttoning her coat.

"Thank you," Cecilia smiled as she took Olivia's coat. "You look..." She trailed off, her eyes expanding slightly as she

THE SECRET COURIER

examined Olivia's form.

"It's from the party last night," Olivia interrupted before Cecilia could continue, straining self-consciously at the cloth that clung to her hips.

"Well, it looks lovely," Cecilia murmured, motioning for Olivia to sit in her normal seat on the couch.

"Thank you," she said meekly, a flush crawling up her neck and onto her cheeks.

"We have some news," Cecilia said, her tone more serious now. "I was going to wait for Harold to tell you, but he's gotten held up and won't be able to join us this week."

"What is it?" She inquired; her brow furrowed.

"The information on the transports you gave us last week," Cecilia said, taking a seat across from Olivia. "Harold passed it along to headquarters and a plan is being made to intercept the supplies as we speak."

"That's wonderful!" Olivia responded, her eyes widening with astonishment. She hadn't expected the travel dates and places she sent Harold last week to arrive in England so swiftly.

"We'll have to wait to hear the outcome of course, considering the first transport isn't scheduled for another two weeks," she

THE SECRET COURIER

said. "But I think our chances of success are pretty high - thanks to you," she continued with a grin.

"Oh," Olivia said, shaking her head. "I'm sure someone else would've gotten their hands on the information if I hadn't been able to."

"Take credit where credit is due." Cecilia grinned, "The only way we were ever getting our hands on information like that was through someone in your position."

Olivia blushed slightly. She had been used to being chastised at her weekly sessions with Harold and Cecilia, whether for anything she did or did not do. Being complimented for her efforts was completely new to her. She enjoyed the sensation it gave her... The sense that she was making a difference in this terrible conflict, that she wasn't squandering her father's effort.

"I know Harold's been hard on you these last few weeks," Cecilia began after a while, shattering the stillness that had enveloped the room.

"He cares for you though, even though he'd never admit it out loud."

"What do you mean?" She inquired, her brow furrowing in perplexity.

"Harold got to know your father well during the year he worked for the service," she said.

171

"I had no idea they had even met," Olivia said.

"Harold considered him a friend," Cecilia said, nodding. "When we received word that he'd..." She trailed off uncomfortably. "Harold took it quite hard."

"I had no idea," Olivia said.

"When you came to us wanting to take your father's place, Harold wouldn't even entertain the idea," she said. "If he'd had his way, you'd have gotten on that ship with your sister, even if he had to force you to." She giggled, a little grin flitting over her lips.

"Why didn't he?" She asked.

"Because of me," Cecilia said honestly. "I told him that I thought it was a good idea for you to stay," she said, perplexed by Olivia's look.

"Why?" She inquired; her interest palpable.

"I know how helpless it feels to stand by while people you care about are taken away from you," Cecilia said, leaning slightly forward in her chair. "You wanted to fight and make a difference. You remind me a lot of myself in that regard." She smiled gently,

"You and I don't like standing on the sidelines."

"I didn't want to run away," Olivia answered gently. That was the first time she had ever confessed it aloud, but it was correct. She despised feeling powerless. Staying behind was the only way she could regain control and guarantee her father's death was not in vain.

Cecilia nodded, indicating her comprehension. "I know."

24

CHAPTER TWENTY-FOUR

Olivia walked along the War Office corridor; her arms wrapped snugly around the stack of brightly colored file folders she carried to her breast.

She rounded the corner into the main work space and slipped past her desk, dropping down a few documents before continuing. The room was mostly empty by 5 p.m., since the other typists had gone home for the day. Striding across the floor, she slid between the unoccupied desks, making her way to General Sinclair's office, knocked softly on the open door before entering.

"Sir, I have the minutes from today's meetings if you'd like to review- Oh,"

Looking up from the papers in her hands, she paused in mid-sentence, her gaze drawn to Hans, who sat in one of the recliners opposite from General Sinclair.

"Thank you, Ms. Carter," General Sinclair smiled, indicating for her to enter. She walked closer, shifting her eyes between Hans and General Sinclair, and placed the paperwork in his extended palm.

"They're color-coded as usual," she said, her cheeks warming slightly as her gaze met Hans's for a brief time.

"Well, sir," Hans said, his eyes resting on Olivia for a minute before rising to his feet. "I believe I should get going."

"Of course. Thank you, Captain," General Sinclair said. Hans nodded and left through the door, shutting it behind him.

"Ms. Carter," General Sinclair said as Olivia approached the door. She turned around and stared at him eagerly. "A word?" He asked, even though it wasn't a question. She nodded slowly, a knot running through her gut. Was she in any kind of trouble? Had she been found out? Don't be silly, she reasoned. If her cover was revealed, being summoned into her boss's office would be the least of her worries.

THE SECRET COURIER

"Please, sit down," he said, gesturing to the chair Hans had just sat in. Sitting down, she took a long breath.

"I wanted to thank you," he added, a lovely grin spreading over the corners of his mouth. "Thank you for all of your hard work here. It has not gone unnoticed."

"Oh," she muttered, the knot in her stomach relaxing somewhat. "Thank you, sir."

"There are other things..." He started slowly "That has not gone unnoticed." He stopped for a minute, as if considering how to continue. "I saw you and Lieutenant Hayesn at the party last Friday ... As well as around the office these last few weeks."

"Sir-," she started, her cheeks flushed with passion.

"He seems to be taken with you," General Sinclair added, prompting her flush to deepen. "You're with him... Not very much. In fact, he appears to make you quite uncomfortable." He moved in his position, putting his elbows on his desk, then continued.

"I don't normally concern myself with the private affairs of my staff, but if Lieutenant Hayesn is being too forward with you, I can speak with-,"

"That won't be necessary," she said unexpectedly. "I don't want any trouble," she said, seeing his astonished face.

THE SECRET COURIER

"If you're sure," he said, clasping his hands together.

"I am," she confirmed with a nod. "Lieutenant Hayesn is quite persistent, but he's harmless."

"I also noticed Captain Friedrich and yourself at the party," General Sinclair said, a knowing grin on his face now.

"Sir, I-," She shook her head, ready to counter any insinuations that were going to be made.

"Captain Friedrich has already informed me about the nature of your relationship," he added, lifting his hand to silence her complaints. He did not look furious or disapproving, as she expected. In fact, he seemed amused, with his lips twisted into a faint grin.

"And was insistent that it would not interfere with either of your duties here at the War Office," he said, his sneer growing.

"Of course, not sir," She shook her head, the warmth that had filled her cheeks spreading down her neck as well. "I'm sorry ... For not being honest."

"It's quite alright," General Sinclair said, shaking his head. He grinned sweetly, his gaze staying on her for longer than they had before. "You know," he said, shattering the hush that had enveloped the room.

"I have a daughter about your age," he said, smiling affectionately. "You remind me of her... Just as smart and

THE SECRET COURIER

resilient."

"That's very kind of you to say, sir," Olivia said, smiling back.

"Well..." He cleared his throat.

"Despite what you may believe, I did not summon you here just to congratulate you on your personal achievements. I was wondering if you would consider attending the security briefings. It would be a significant addition to your already heavy workload, but the meetings may benefit from some of your organizing skills."

"Of course, sir," Olivia said, attempting to hide her amazement.

"I'll speak with Mr. Mills and let him know you'll be busy in the afternoon now," General Sinclair remarked, rising to his feet and offering a hand to Olivia.

"Thank you, sir," she said, shaking his offered hand.

***

"What did the General wish to speak with you about?" Hans inquired nonchalantly, moving himself off the brick face where he had been waiting for her. Striding beside Olivia, they descended the War Office's front steps.

"I suppose you already know, don't you?" She raised an eyebrow at him but did not turn her head to face him. "You could've

THE SECRET COURIER

consulted with me before spilling all of our secrets to General Sinclair, you know?" She continued, attempting to hide the grin on the corners of her lips as they strolled side by side along the sidewalk.

"I suppose it was a bit reckless of me," Hans conceded.

He grabbed her hand and took her into an empty alleyway, away from the main road. "But I want you... all of you," he replied, looking down at her.

"You have all of me," she said, the cold brick against her back and his gaze on her sending shivers down her spine.

"I know." He grabbed her other hand in his and pulled them together, kissing both of them lightly before laying them on his chest. "But I'd want to hold your hand while we go down the sidewalk. I want to take you out to supper without fearing that someone from the workplace will see us. I want to kiss you. And not only when we're alone," he said, placing his hands on her hips.

"You could kiss me right now," she whispered quietly, brushing her fingertips on his chest. "Seeing as the secret's out."

"I suppose I could," he said, their noses almost touching now. He brushed his lips teasingly against hers, the brief contact sending a million small electric shocks through her system. His lips moved against her jaw and down her neck, never pausing to

THE SECRET COURIER

place a kiss. She closed her eyes, his warm breath across her skin a startling contrast to the frigid winter air.

"Let me walk you home," he murmured to her ear, his grasp on her hips tightening slightly.

She nodded knowingly, taking a long breath to calm herself. He released her waist and grabbed her hand, guiding her back onto the pavement.

***

"General Sinclair asked me if I'd start attending the security briefings," Olivia added, placing a finger across Hans's belly scar.

"Really?" Hans answered, caressing her hair as he had done for the last half hour. "Well, they could certainly be more organized, and that appears to be your specialty," he said, twisting one of her locks around his finger. "He likes you; you know."

"Who?" She inquired, moving her head off his chest to properly gaze at him.

"The General," he said matter-of-factly. "The men in those meetings are handpicked... They are men General Sinclair trusts. Being invited to attend indicates that he thinks highly of you."

"You sound surprised," she said, raising an eyebrow at him.

"Not in the least," he grinned, sliding his fingers down her naked back. "You have an impact on everyone you encounter...

THE SECRET COURIER

They couldn't help but like you."

"Well, not everyone," she said, putting her arms over his chest and resting her head on them.

"Mr. Mills doesn't seem too keen on me."

"Franklin Mills is intimidated by you, and any other woman not afraid to speak her mind for that matter," Hans said with a smirk.

She laughed. "Well, you're quite charming yourself," she grinned, turning totally over and landing on top of him. "You did persuade me to let you take me out after all," she said, her smile growing. She propped her elbows on his shoulders and rested her cheek on her knuckles. He gripped her waist and pushed her over onto the bed, putting his body on top of hers.

"That was dumb luck," he said, softly touching her face and pressing his chest against hers. He looked down at her, and none of them said anything.

"What I said... About thinking I love you," he added after a pause. "I meant it."

"So did I," she said genuinely. And she did. She was falling in love with Hans Friedrich.

25

CHAPTER TWENTY-FIVE

"Are you coming?" Hans's voice came from the other side of her desk. Olivia glanced up from her keyboard, her fingers still hammering furiously on the keys, and smiled at Hans.

"Just finishing up this..." She trailed off, her eyes falling back down to type the final few characters on the sheet of notes she had been copying. "Page," she eventually ended her sentence, sliding over the type carriage on the typewriter, pulling her chair back, and rising to her feet. She zipped up the typewriter's case and took it with her as she and Hans walked down the long corridor to the conference room where meetings were

THE SECRET COURIER

conducted.

"Are you sure this is a good idea? Are we walking in together?" When they approached the door, she turned to face him. It was her first day of security briefings and her first day back at work since their relationship became known. She didn't want General Sinclair to have any doubts about her capacity to separate work and pleasure.

"You could go in a few seconds before me," Hans replied with an amused sneer on his lips. "If it'd make you feel better."

"Well wouldn't that look a bit staged?" She spoke earnestly. "Like we meant not to come in together?"

"Olivia..." He paused, grasping her hand in his. "You're overthinking it." His sneer grew as he pushed against the door, dragging her inside. "Come on." He let go of her hand and moved to their separate places around the table, Olivia at General Sinclair's right hand and Hans a few seats down.

"Let's get started," General Sinclair remarked, rising to his feet once the final guy came and took his seat. "Gentlemen, Ms. Carter will be attending all of our meetings from now on," he said, nodding toward Olivia. "I dare say with a bit more structure, we could all be home by four o'clock each afternoon."

"I'm all for that," Lieutenant Hayesn said, his gaze fixed on Olivia and a tiny grin on his lips.

183

THE SECRET COURIER

She averted her gaze, warmth spreading over her cheeks as his gaze lingered on her.

"Yes, well," said General Sinclair, clearing his mouth. "Lieutenant Hayes, why don't you start us off."

"Of course, sir," Lieutenant Hayes said, the sneer still visible on his face, but Olivia dared not glance up from her keyboard. "The labor camps have worked ceaselessly. The supply total as of yesterday was 800 pounds of food and 200 boxes of ammunition from our facilities."

"Good," said General Sinclair, nodding. "Shultz, what word from Berlin?"

"They'll be expecting our shipment on January ninth, sir," said the same tall, slender guy she recognized from the morning meetings, pulling his cotton top hair off his forehead while reading from the page in front of him.

"Men will be stationed at the border at Bocholt to accept supplies and carry them to Essen. The cargoes are still scheduled to be flown to Berlin and ultimately to Stalingrad."

The conference stretched on, and the men in the room discussed the exact munitions supplied by the manufacturers in Den Haag, as well as whether or not to convey the supplies by

THE SECRET COURIER

military vehicle.

Olivia transcribed every word, taking mental notes on everything spoken in preparation for her appointment with Harold and Cecilia.

According to the paper she had seen on General Sinclair's desk, the plan had not changed, and she was relieved that the information she had given Harold and Cecilia was still applicable... especially since preparations to intercept the supplies had already been formed.

"Alright boys," General Sinclair replied after the final man had delivered his report. "Let's call it a day, shall we?" The soldiers around the table started packing up their belongings, placing file folders into satchels and putting jackets over their uniforms in readiness to leave the warm confines of the War Office and into the frigid December weather.

"If the remainder of the week goes this well, we'll get Friday afternoon off... Let you all have a head start on your Christmas vacation," General Sinclair grinned, gentle murmuring filling the room as the troops filed out.

"Ms. Carter," General Sinclair turned to face her. "If you'd be willing to type these up and make enough copies for everyone, I'd be grateful," he continued, giving General Sinclair the

185

THE SECRET COURIER

reports each soldier had handed him before leaving.

"Of course, sir," she said, taking the folders from him. She started packing her belongings by tucking them under her arm.

She departed the room after zipping up her typewriter case and heaving it off the table. As she made her way down the corridor to the workroom, her gaze was drawn to Hans, who was leaning against her desk. She grinned coyly as she approached him.

"Do you have plans tonight?" He inquired, removing her typewriter case and setting it on the desk for her.

"I have a date," she said, grinning at his perplexed gaze. "With these," she said, holding up the reports that General Sinclair had handed her.

"I figured you'd say that," He remarked, lifting a sly brow. Pushing himself away from the area he'd been resting against, he took a chair from another desk and moved it near Olivia's, plopping down with a smug look. "Mind if I tag along?"

"Well, it seems you've already made yourself at home, so I suppose not," she responded, mirroring his sneer. "No distractions, though," she continued, giving him a look that indicated she meant it.

"I'll be on my best behavior," he added, holding out his palms to simulate innocence. She rolled her eyes and sat down, preparing

THE SECRET COURIER

her typewriter for what would be a long evening. She opened the first report in the stack of files and started typing, copying each word onto the special waxed paper she'd need to create copies.

They sat in quiet for a moment, with Olivia's fingers tapping on the typewriter keys making the only sound in the empty room. She looked at Hans from the corner of her eye as she turned over a finished page. He was thumbing through the copy of Bleak House she had in her desk, despite the fact that she hadn't taken it up in weeks, since she was too busy to enjoy any recreational reading.

"Have you ever read it?" She inquired, gesturing to the book in Hans's hands.

He nodded. "I was never much of a fan, though," He added, shutting the book and turning it over in his hands as if to study it. "I've always thought it really sad... How much heartache might have been saved if there hadn't been so many secrets. Take Esther, for example," he said, setting the book down on the desk.

"She knew how she felt about Mr. Woodcourt, and how he felt about her, but she waited years to admit it."

"She couldn't be honest with Mr. Woodcourt," Olivia said, shaking her head. "Her circumstances wouldn't have allowed it."

THE SECRET COURIER

She averted her gaze, realizing for the first time how much she resembled Dickens' main character. "Besides, they found each other in the end."

"I guess so," Hans said, shrugging. "But think about how much more time they would've had together had they not been so preoccupied with other people's perception of them."

"Sometimes the way people see you is the only perception that matters," she remarked, holding Hans's gaze.

"I suppose you're right," he murmured, maintaining her stare. He leaned forward in his chair, his elbows resting on his knees. "Do you want to know what I see when I look at you?" He inquired, his gaze examining every detail of her face.

"What?" She questioned, turning in her seat to face him, a little grin on her lips.

"I see the smartest," He stopped, stroking a strand of hair from her face. "Most driven," he said, moving his palm down her face and resting it on her jaw. "Most beautiful woman I've ever met," he said, putting his forehead on hers. He leaned in and kissed her lightly, then pulled away after a few agonizingly brief seconds. "I thought I said no distractions," she grinned, unable to break away from his contact.

"I gave it my all," he said slyly, matching her grin.

"Well, I suppose a short break wouldn't hurt anything," she murmured, laying another quick kiss on his lips.

"Agreed."

26

CHAPTER TWENTY-SIX

"What's this?" Olivia wrinkled her brow, looking between Hans

THE SECRET COURIER

and the brown bundle wrapped with thread that he carried in his extended palm.

He had volunteered to make a Christmas Eve supper for her, and she had agreed, relieved not to be spending the holiday alone with her thoughts. They had finished their meal and were now relaxing on the couch, sipping whiskey and listening to quiet jazz from the record player in the corner of the room.

"Your Christmas gift," Hans grinned as he took her drink and replaced it with the box.

"I thought we weren't buying each other gifts?" She lifted an inquisitive eyebrow.

"Well, I didn't buy it," he said, smirking. "Just open it," he said after she gave him another glance.

"Alright, alright," she chuckled as she untied the thread around the parcel. Tearing apart the paper, her gaze landed on the book within. "Great Expectations," she said, reading the title out loud.

"It's my favorite Dickens book," Hans said with a grin. "I wrote to my mother and asked her to look for it in my room at home. She discovered it and sent it to me."

"How long have you been planning this?" She inquired, looking between Hans and the book in her hands.

"Since I saw you at work, reading in the break room," he said with a laugh. "Christmas just seemed like an appropriate time to give it to you," he said with a smirk.

"Well, now I feel bad for not having you anything," she said with a small grimace.

"I have everything I want right here," he said, smiling at her. He leaned in, placed his forehead against hers, and gave her a short kiss on the lips.

"Your favorite Dickens book, huh?" She inquired, a slight grin raising the corners of her lips.

"Mhm," he said, nodding against her forehead.

"Yet Bleak House is too sad for you?" She inquired, her smile broadening as she drew back to look at him properly.

"I've always found Pip and Estella's story... redemptive," he chuckled, despite his somber tone. "Both grew. Pip- due of his good fortune; Estella- despite her misery... Pip's forgiveness ultimately teaches her how to love."

"I've never thought about it that way," she said gently. "I suppose she's right, though, suffering has been stronger than all other teaching," she added, citing Estella from the novel.

"And has taught me to understand what your heart used to be," Hans said, ending the quotation.

"You never cease to amaze me," she said, shaking her head.

THE SECRET COURIER

"You're so..."

"Not a complete imbecile?" Hans grinned.

"I was going to say well read," Olivia giggled.

"Well, there wasn't much else to do on slow days at my parents' store, but to read," he said with a smirk.

"My father had a huge library in his office above the shop. I recall going upstairs and selecting a book to read as I sat at the cash register. I read this one so many times that he ended up giving it to me," He added, touching the book on Olivia's lap.

"Well, thank you for giving it to me," she said, smiling.

"Of course," he said, smiling back. Leaning forward, he slipped his hand off the book and onto her knee.

Her eyes met his, which were black with something that sent shivers down her spine. She closed her eyes, her lips touching his as she blindly put the book on the side table. Sliding his hand up, he clasped her waist, his lips leaving hers and meeting with her neck.

"Stay here tonight," he whispered, putting a gentle kiss on her earlobe. She nodded. Taking the hand that grabbed her waist, she rose up, dragging Hans from the couch and into his room. He let go of her hand and grabbed her waist, lifting her off the ground and over his shoulder in one rapid movement.

"Hey! Put me down," she joked, smacking his back as he carried her along the corridor. Her back banged against the bed when he slung her off his shoulder. "That wasn't very gentlemanly," she smirked, supporting herself on her elbows.

"I can't always be a gentleman," he said with a smile, jumping onto the bed. She giggled, wrapping her arms around his neck and pressing a kiss on his lips.

"Merry Christmas, Hans," she whispered, drawing aside to stare at him, their eyes connecting.

"Merry Christmas Olivia."

27

CHAPTER TWENTY-SEVEN

"I trust you had a good holiday?" General Sinclair inquired, glancing up from his papers as Olivia entered the meeting room.

"Oh, yes, sir," she said with a grin. "Thank you."

She had spent the whole holiday weekend with Hans, only leaving momentarily for a meeting with the Winslows. Their discussion was brief, with no fresh information to share and no word on intentions to intercept the trucks. Cecilia had given her every leftover in the fridge from the previous day's Christmas meal, so she departed with a full tummy and a tin of cinnamon bread in less than an hour.

"Did you spend it with family?" General Sinclair inquired casually.

"I'm afraid not," she said, shaking her head. "No family around to spend it with," she shrugged at General Sinclair's perplexed expression.

THE SECRET COURIER

"I'm sorry," he said knowingly, furrowing his brow. "I didn't realize."

"It happened so long ago," she claimed, dismissing his concerns. "My sister writes from England," she said, knowing she hadn't and wouldn't be getting a letter from Grace anytime soon.

She despised it when others pitied her for losing her parents and brother. They gave her concerned glances, with their brows screwed up and their mouths turned down into frowns. Each time, all it did was twist the knife buried deep inside her chest. She wanted someone to look at her normally.

Her thoughts drifted to Hans. He'd always treated her normally, never pitying her for all she'd lost... perhaps because he understood all too well how it felt to be the target of sympathetic looks.

She was distracted from her thoughts by the sound of the conference room door sliding shut. She glanced up, her gaze fixed on Lieutenant Hayesn. As he neared, whatever happy look on her face evaporated.

"Good morning, sir," Lieutenant Hayesn said to General Sinclair. "Ms. Carter," he grinned at her, his gaze lingering on hers for too long. She nodded automatically before rising and beginning to put out an agenda for each seat at the meeting table. "I have that report you asked for, sir," Lieutenant Hayesn remarked,

THE SECRET COURIER

giving General Sinclair the folder he was holding.

"Thank you, Lieutenant," said General Sinclair, nodding. "Be safe on your trip," he said, shaking Lieutenant Hayesn's hand.

'Trip?' Olivia thought to herself. Was he on vacation or going on official business? She had not heard anything about the trip at any of the meetings.

"Thank you, sir," Lieutenant Hayesn grinned, peeking at Olivia from the corner of his eye. "I'll be anxiously awaiting my return to the War Office." With that, he turned on his heel and left the meeting room.

"Would you like me to make copies of that sir?" Olivia inquired, referring to the paperwork that Lieutenant Hayesn had given General Sinclair.

"Oh, no," said General Sinclair, shaking his head. "We won't be discussing it in the meeting today," he remarked, putting the folder under the stack of papers in front of him.

His genial smile never wavered.

"Alright," she agreed, mirroring his kind grin, but she had a hunch there was more to the tale than General Sinclair was revealing.

It had never occurred to her that any of the sessions, even the

THE SECRET COURIER

security briefings, may not include all of the pertinent material. Was it a routine report from the work camps, or something more vital intended just for the General's eyes? Lieutenant Hayesn said he had asked it... He undoubtedly demanded hundreds of reports from the officers under his command. Still, she couldn't ignore the nagging sensation in her stomach that she wanted to examine whatever was in that file.

***

"Where is Lieutenant Hayesn going?" Olivia inquired, striving to maintain a casual tone. She was sitting on Hans's bed, with the book of Great Exceptions he had given her for Christmas open across her lap, though she hadn't been reading it. Her thoughts had been busy all day with the dossier Lieutenant Hayesn had handed General Sinclair that morning. As the General had said, there had been no discussion of the file's contents that day, but she was convinced she had seen him open it when he returned to his office after the morning meeting, only to quickly close his door behind him.

"I believe he's headed up north to the labor camp in Amersfoort," Hans said, unbuckling his jeans and sliding them off before coming into bed in only his boxers and a white t-shirt. "Why?"

THE SECRET COURIER

"Just curious," Olivia shrugged. "There just wasn't any mention of his trip in the meetings."

"I am sure this is simply a normal appointment... Not much to write home about," he grinned.

"You're probably right," she grinned, but her instincts warned her there was something more.

"Are you ready for bed?" Hans inquired, raising himself up on one elbow.

"I think I'm going to read in the living room for a while," she said, bringing up the book from her lap. "I don't want to keep you up," she said as his brow wrinkled.

"Alright," he said. "Don't stay gone too long," he said, clutching her hand as she rose out of bed.

"I won't," she grinned, bending in to kiss Hans on the lips before heading for the door, leaving it cracked open behind her. She had little interest in reading. It was all part of the spontaneous plan she had devised in her brain after attempting to sneak a short glimpse at the file General Sinclair had left on his desk earlier that day, only to find his office door unusually closed.

Her idea, as ridiculous as it seemed, was to break into the War Office. Not a true break-in. She would have a key, namely Hans's key.

THE SECRET COURIER

Hans had spent the last several days coming in early and working late to catch up on the heaps of work that had accumulated over the long weekend. It had left him tired. That tiredness, along with the few too many glasses of Scotch he had consumed to relax, meant all she had to do was wait for him to fall asleep...

Which probably wouldn't take long. Then she'd steal his key and sneak out to the War Office, returning herself and the key before he realized they were gone.

Sitting on the couch, she cuddled up beneath a blanket, her eyes skimming the pages of her book as she replayed the plan in her thoughts. After a half-hour, she closed the book and placed it on the side table before getting to her feet.

She crept down the hallway, peeping through the breach she had made in Hans's bedroom door. He lay in bed, his mouth wide, snoring loudly against his pillow. She smiled and watched him for a few more seconds to be sure he was indeed sleeping.

Tiptoeing back down the hallway, she snatched his uniform coat off the back of the couch and rummaged through the pockets, revealing a ring of silver keys. She put on her coat, pocketed them, and went for the door. She slung her bag over her shoulder and grabbed her heels from the floor by the door, figuring it was better to put them on once outside. As she

THE SECRET COURIER

turned the handle, the door opened and closed quietly, allowing her to go out into the night.

To be continued in Part II......

Author Note

Thank you for reading one of my books. This is my 4th book. I would love to hear your honest opinion about the book in a review/suggestion for me to read. I wish to make improvements in subsequent books based and make my work more appreciable to you and others.

If you enjoyed this novel, I have recommended more of my books in the next page. The part II of this novel has also been released; you can find it in the store.

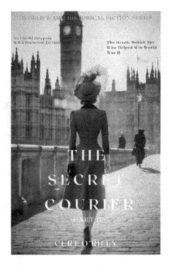

Recommended Reads

WORLD WAR II HOLOCAUST FICTION SERIES

Forbidden Bonds of Auschwitz (Book 1)

Forbidden Bonds of Auschwitz (Book 2)

The Warsaw Reistance

The Secret Courier (Book 1)

The Secret Courier (Book 2)

War's Embrace

A Silent Heart

I Am Daliah

About The Author

I am a storyteller with a knack for finding the extraordinary in everyday life. Hailing from a small town, I bring a down-to-earth charm to the world of fiction, where relatable characters navigate the twists and turns of life in compelling and authentic ways.

I draw inspiration from the simplicity of my small-town living and the complexity of human relationships, I try to make my stories resonate with readers who appreciate the beauty found in the ordinary. With a writing style that is approachable and engaging, I have crafted narratives that capture the essence of the human experience.

Whether exploring the dynamics of family, delving into the challenges of modern relationships, or simply observing the quirks of daily life, my stories are grounded in a realism that makes them both accessible and compelling.

Printed in the USA
CPSIA information can be obtained
at www.ICGtesting.com
LVHW090809210924
791741LV00029B/223